W9-CDO-018

THE SILKEN THREAD

THE SILKEN THREAD

Judith Saxton

G.K. Hall & Co. • Chivers Press
Thorndike, Maine USA   Bath, England

This Large Print edition is published by G.K. Hall & Co., USA and by Chivers Press, England.

Published in 2000 in the U.S. by arrangement with Chivers Press Limited.

Published in 2000 in the U.K. by arrangement with Severn House Publishers Ltd.

U.S. Hardcover   0-7838-9040-0   (Romance Series Edition)
U.K.Hardcover   0-7540-4180-8   (Chivers Large Print)
U.K.Softcover   0-7540-4181-6   (Camden Large Print)

Originally published 1981 under the title *Triple Triangle* and pseudonym *Judy Turner*.

The text of this Large Print edition is unabridged.
Other aspects of the book may vary from the original edition.

Set in 16 pt. Plantin by Anne Bradeen.

Printed in the United States on permanent paper.

British Library Cataloguing-in-Publication Data available

Library of Congress Cataloging-in-Publication Data

Saxton, Judith, 1936 –
     [Triple triangle]
     The silken thread / Judith Saxton.
        p. cm.
     "Originally published 1981 under the title Triple triangle and pseudonym Judy Turner" — T.p. verso.
     ISBN 0-7838-9040-0 (lg. print : hc : alk. paper)
     1. Large type books.   I. Title.
PR6069.A97 S56 2000
823´.914—dc21   00-029571

THE SILKEN THREAD

CHAPTER ONE

'If it were up to me you might go and welcome, Vanessa, but it is not! Mr Frederick Talbot is your legal guardian and he's adamant. When you're eighteen he says he'll take you to London and present you at court, give a ball for you, do everything that is proper, but not until then. And really dear, it's unkind to glower at me, for I'm powerless to change his mind.'

Mrs Nessie Mordred, a plump little woman with frizzed hair and a goodnatured though foolish face, looked pleadingly at her niece, but Vanessa Bascombe continued to eye her aunt smoulderingly.

She was a slim girl with an abundance of bright, copper-red curls dressed *à la Chinoise* and tied with a flowered ribbon. She wore a fashionable sack dress with its rich satin train heavily embroidered, a bell hoop accentuated her small waist, and the toes peeping from beneath her petticoat were encased in the latest fashion in

7

French satin shoes. Her small, heart-shaped face would have been pretty, but at present it was marred by a scowl which drew her soft brows close and tightened her lips into a straight line.

'Tell him I'm very old for my years; more like eighteen than seventeen! Tell him that by then I shall be dead of boredom, shut away in the country with no company other than that of my cousin! Tell him . . . Tell him I *shall* go!'

Aunt Nessie glanced helplessly towards the third occupant of the blue salon. The young woman thus appealed to, a handsome brunette of about twenty, put down her book, got to her feet, and came over to her mother and cousin. She sat down on the gold satin sofa, smiled at the combatants, and patted the cushions on each side of her.

'Come and sit down, and let's discuss the matter sensibly, and with a little less heat, cousin! You know Mama is speaking the truth when she says she cannot persuade Mr Talbot to allow you to visit your Godmama for the Season, so why not agree to wait a year?'

Vanessa sank on to the sofa and twisted round to face her cousin.

'Rhoda, *darling* Rhoda, it's so unfair and stuffy to insist on waiting until I'm eighteen! I've been to parties here, I went to the O'Neill's betrothal ball when his lordship invited us, and to Pamela Courtney's masquerade! Several young men treated me with flattering attention, and no one said I was too young to attend!'

'Oh Vanessa, that's not true! You told me afterwards that Pamela's admirer said he'd not realised it was to be a nursery party, or he would have brought his six-year-old cousin!'

This reminder earned a look of deep loathing from Vanessa.

'Jerome Harcourt! Huh! He was annoyed because Pamela and I were talking and he wanted all her attention. He's abominable, and self-satisfied, and I can't think why Pamela wants to marry him!'

'He's a handsome rake with a great deal of charm. That's why.'

'Oh Rhoda, I don't find him charming. I think he's . . .'

'You've already aired your opinion,' Rhoda said blandly. 'Now Van, dear, you've admitted you enjoy country parties; why not continue to enjoy them this year, and challenge the metropolis next year?'

'Because the chance won't come again, and I won't turn it down,' Vanessa said, her scowl descending once more. 'If I don't go this time my Godmama will never invite me again, and I've no wish to be brought out by the Talbots. They're mean and they're fault-finders, and they want to bring me out next year for their own selfish reasons.'

Aunt Nessie, sitting quietly at her daughter's other side, thought hopefully that the worst of Vanessa's rage seemed to be over. Now she might see reason. It was that red hair, she reflected. It really did seem to make its owner susceptible to tantrums!

'That may be true, cousin, but why do you think the Talbots won't let you visit Lady Harrison?'

'Because they've got that sharp-nosed daughter to bring out next year, and they hope to save money by letting her share my parties. After all, it's my own money which will fire *me* off, not Mr Talbot's!'

'Vanessa, that wasn't kind,' Aunt Nessie tried to sound shocked but it was difficult, since she had a shrewd suspicion that her niece had hit the nail on the head.

'I'm not kind, am I?' Vanessa giggled. 'What's more, the Talbots hope their son may win me if I'm living in their house for months and months.'

'If Captain Talbot makes you an offer you have only to refuse,' Aunt Nessie pointed out.

'And if he lives under the same roof as you for months and months, and still wants to marry you, he's a hero and you should be *proud* to marry him,' Rhoda observed.

Aunt Nessie braced herself for an explosion of fury from her niece, but it did not come. Vanessa had a sense of humour, and knew her own failings.

'I know what you mean! But some men would marry anyone for money, and you must admit I'm monstrously rich — filthy rich, in fact!'

10

'Vanessa! That was vulgar, and coarse, and . . .'

Rhoda interrupted her mother. 'That's not all, there's another reason why Mr Talbot won't consider this invitation. Tell her, Mama.'

Aunt Nessie leaned across and patted her niece's knee.

'The truth is, dear, that Mr Talbot and Lady Harrison have been on bad terms for years, ever since she married Everard Harrison in fact. That's why she very improperly approached you directly with the invitation. But of course I had to ask your guardian's consent and he wrote back at once to say you may not go, and that you must write to Lady Harrison yourself, telling her that you will be brought out next year, under Mr Talbot's aegis.'

'I didn't know that,' Vanessa said slowly. She got to her feet and crossed the room, standing in the window embrasure and looking out across the pleasure gardens which surrounded Bascombe Hall. It was a bitterly cold day, but snowdrops were clustered beneath the leafless copper beech which grew in the middle of the wide lawn and already the daffodils were spearing through the soil with their promise of spring to come.

'So you see, dear, there really is nothing we can do,' Aunt Nessie said, joining her niece by the window. 'Gracious, how dark the sky is! I shouldn't be surprised if we had some snow.'

'You're right, Aunt.' Vanessa looked mournful. 'I'll go to my room now and write to Lady Harrison, but I'll write to Mr Talbot as well and tell him what I think. Then I'll change into my new riding habit — the one made of dark green broadcloth, Rhoda — and ride into the village with the letters. Would you care to accompany me, coz?'

'No thank you, it's too cold for riding,' Rhoda said. 'In fact, your mention of riding habits reminds me that I've not yet mended the tear in my petticoat which I did last week. And I want to make a lace ruff to wear with my ball gown, because there's an Assembly ball on Tuesday next and since Mr Tallow will be back from Newcastle by then, I hope to attend it with his escort.' Rhoda was betrothed to Mr Tallow, a respectable young merchant whose money made him eligible to the Mordreds. She smiled affectionately at her cousin now, and crossed the blue carpet to stand beside her. 'You're being sensible, Van, and that shows more than anything how fast you are leaving childish things behind and becoming a young lady.'

'I suppose you're right,' Vanessa said ruefully. 'I don't mean to be unreasonable and difficult, but . . .'

'But you can't help it,' Rhoda said, smiling. 'I remember being seventeen and bored to death with the country! Now, here's a thought! Mr Tallow was telling me before he left that he would be bringing back his cousin to stay for a while. I believe he is a year or so older than you; how would it be if Mr Tallow's cousin came to the assembly to dance attendance upon you?'

'That would be nice,' Vanessa said politely. Such politeness at the mention of Mr Tallow might have made Rhoda wonder what was going on in Vanessa's head, for her cousin had more than once denounced the worthy Mr Tallow as a boring bumpkin, but her recent betrothal made her assume that everyone now viewed that gentleman through the same rosy spectacles as she herself wore.

An hour later, had she seen a figure wrapped in a long cloak and carrying a bundle slip out of the house and head for the stables, she would merely have concluded that her cousin was taking her letters to the village, along with a bundle of mending for the sewing woman.

If she had known that Vanessa was clad in young Charlie Mordred's coat and second-best breeches, and that a purse filled with her own mother's next month's pin-money adorned her belt, she would have been horrified. But since she neither saw Vanessa leave the house nor visited her room for many hours, she remained in happy ignorance that the younger girl was on her way to London, regardless of guardians, aunts, or indeed, of the proprieties!

Jerome Harcourt, sitting moodily over breakfast in the small parlour at Harcourt Manor, glanced outside at the threatening grey clouds and groaned.

'Look at that sky! No chance of hunting if we

have snow! Is there any post for me, Mincing?'

Mincing, valet, friend and general factotum to the owner of the mouldering splendour of the Harcourt estate said blandly, 'Yes, sir. Leaning against the marmalade pot, sir.'

Jerome reached for the letter and knocked against the coffee pot, which responded with a single, high note. Jerome's hand checked for a moment and he drew in his breath and screwed up his eyes, then he reached again for the letter.

'Head bad this morning, sir?' Mincing asked sympathetically, as his employer slit the letter open and scanned the contents through screwed-up eyelids, before tossing it down on the table once more and lifting his tankard of ale to his lips.

'*Yes*, confound you! What a welcome my Mama handed out when I arrived last night though, enough to drive anyone to drink! She really thought Miss Courtney as good as won, and her fortune about to become Harcourt property.' He grimaced, drained his ale, and set the tankard down on the table with exaggerated caution. 'And so she would have been — mine, I mean — if her father hadn't announced that the match was "unsuitable", as soon as I popped the question!'

'Naturally, Mrs Harcourt was upset then, sir. Your happiness . . .'

'Ha! Much she cared about my happiness! She flew at me, accusing me of deliberately ruining

14

my chances of the marriage by carrying on with some little chit . . .' He shrugged, reaching once more for the letter. 'So when she finally left me last night, I drowned my sorrows in the brandy my father laid down for special occasions. If you ask me, he was cheated, for never have I had a head like it! Now, let's take a look at this letter! It's from my uncle, Sir Thomas Remington, which means it's not a dunning epistle, at least.'

He scanned the letter, then pushed back his chair and stood up, glancing towards the window.

'What do you think of the weather, Mincing? This letter is certainly interesting. How long would it take us to get ready to leave this place, d'you think?'

'Should we say two hours, sir?' Mincing, no country lover, allowed a gratified smile to play about his thin features. He had not thought they would rusticate for long, not with Mr Harcourt's Mama in residence! 'May I ask why you are considering leaving the Manor so soon, sir?'

Jerome strolled over to the window, tapping the letter thoughtfully against his thigh.

'It's this news, Mincing. Sir Thomas tells me that he is to entertain his wife's god-daughter, Mathilda Randolph, for the London season. She has an elderly Papa but no Mama, and my uncle and aunt have offered to stand in loco parentis during her first season.' He grinned at Mincing's unmoved countenance. 'I should, perhaps, add

15

that she is a considerable heiress, being her Papa's one and only child.'

'And Sir Thomas suggests you move back to London?'

'He does. No doubt she's plain as a pikestaff, but pretty women are a luxury a man in my position can't afford! He hopes, of course, that I may win her heart. And her fortune.'

Mincing coughed. 'But how, sir, if I may make so bold, does your uncle expect you to win the young lady's heart? Or rather, what difference will it make if you do? Fathers, by and large, are strangely indifferent to your charm and address.'

'That's a home-thrust, man! But apparently this Papa simply dotes on his child, and Sir Thomas hopes that, if I manage to make her fall deep in love, and behave with unusual circumspection, her Papa may consent to the marriage sooner than see his daughter go into a decline.'

'That means, I assume, that you must give up gambling, horse racing, expensive mistresses . . .'

'Damme, man, I've already started to cut my coat according to my cloth! Didn't you notice that the sweet Dinah has gone into other keeping? It cost me a pang to part with her, but we'd been together for several months.' He grinned at the disapproval on his manservant's countenance. 'Look, man, if I land myself an heiress, I shall be able to put this place to rights.' He continued to contemplate the ruin of the rose garden beyond the glass, his harsh expression softening. 'I was happy here once, and so were you. When my father was alive, and my eldest brother Philip. Do you remember how the place buzzed with servants, how the farms were all productive and the tenants content? It could be like that again.' He turned from the window and said, 'Start packing at once, if you please,' then he left the room, and striding across the hall with his head down, cannoned into his Mama, bound for the breakfast parlour.

'Jerome! Do, pray, take care! Where are you off to in such a hurry that you do not even see me?'

Demetria Harcourt was a tall, handsome woman with a nature as passionate as it was selfish. For years she had milked the estate to pay for her pleasures and for those of her son Philip, whom she adored. When Philip had died in a shooting accident and Jerome, then a lad of fourteen, had inherited, she had known that she must either retrench or hand over to her son nothing but debts.

She had, quite coldly and calculatingly, chosen the latter course and had watched with indifference her second son's wild and profligate career until, three years ago, it had been made plain to her both by her son and by his man of business that she must, in future, live on her jointure.

When her first fury had cooled, she had begun to search for a rich wife for Jerome. As a younger woman she had taken lovers but had never attempted to re-marry, enjoying the freedom being a widow gave her. Now, she almost wished she had wed, but it was too late. A handsome but penniless widow with expensive tastes might be offered many things, but a respectable marriage was not one of them.

Jerome had never questioned his mother's morals; his own did not bear close examination. But he did question both her expenditure and her management of the estate. He had been horrified by the extent of her extravagance, and quick to put a stop to it.

Yet though he could not love Demetria, he did admire her. The fact that she could, and did, manage on her drastically curtailed income, her air of elegance and fashion; the ingenuity, even, in which her more extravagant tastes were now indulged only at someone else's expense. It was a reluctant admiration perhaps, but it existed, and made small doses of her company just bearable.

Nevertheless of late he had treated her cautiously for she had only, it seemed, to set eyes on him to start animadverting on the fate which had stolen Philip from her and left her with a worthless son who could not, or would not, marry well and make her comfortable.

Putting out his hands to steady his Mama after their collision, therefore, Jerome said politely: 'I'm sorry Demetria, I was in a brown study. I'm off to London this morning.'

Long ago, she had ordered him to stop calling her Mama; it made her feel old, she said. So now he used her first name, except when he wanted to annoy her.

'London?' Her thin, arched brows shot up. 'I should have thought, Jerome, after the deep disappointment you've . . .'

He cut across her complaining voice without compunction.

'Yes, I know, Mama, I should not have let Miss Courtney and her fortune slip through my fingers; you did mention it last night! But I am being a dutiful son, I assure you. I'm going to London because Sir Thomas and Aunt Maria have a young woman staying with them . . .'

'Ah! Could it be Miss Randolph?'

Jerome's black eyebrows flew up. 'It is. How in heaven's name . . .'

'I make it my business to know all about heiresses, Jerome.' Demetria smiled sweetly up at her tall son. 'I shall accompany you. I'm sure dear Maria would want me to do so.'

'Good God, no! With you looking on . . .'

The smile on Demetria's face did not falter, though it grew a trifle fixed.

'Nonsense, my dear boy. Only look what happened when I left you alone with the Courtney girl! And before that, Miss Seraphina Copland, and before that, Annabel Withers, and before that . . . Bless me, Jerome, if I don't take a hand, you'll become a gazetted fortune hunter, without a chance of an heiress.'

'That was a little vulgar,' murmured Jerome, and had the satisfaction of seeing a look of chagrin cross his mother's face. 'But I suppose I can't stop you going to London. However, not in my company, for I mean to ride. I leave in an hour.'

'I can't do so, of course, for I must order things here first. Well, dear boy, if you leave Mincing with me, I daresay I may set out within two or three days.'

'Certainly,' Jerome said basely, anxious only to avoid his Mama's company for days at a time in a coach and at various coaching inns, for she would, he knew, travel slowly and with many stops. Remembering the grey clouds, he added without much hope: 'Though we're in for bad weather, I fear, and you know how you hate travelling in the snow.'

She patted his arm, then glided towards the breakfast parlour once more.

'For your sake, Jerome, I'll even risk snow.'

Jerome strode across the hall and up the stairs towards his own bedchamber. He wondered whether it might be possible to stop Demetria's visit by begging Uncle Thomas to maintain that the house was full. He himself would live in his lodgings, but would visit the Remington house daily to ingratiate himself with their fair guest.

However, it was no use worrying about it, and in any event he could not imagine Sir Thomas turning his own sister from his door, however much he might disapprove of Demetria. And he knew from his uncle's letter that the heiress would not be arriving at the house in Hanover Square for two or three days. Perhaps, if he could keep Demetria from actually monopolising Miss Randolph and ruining all, he might find himself marrying money at last!

Jerome, bending low over his stallion's neck, felt the first snow kiss his face before he had ridden ten miles. Glancing up at the laden clouds, he wondered whether to turn back, then decided against it. If he did, Demetria would claim his escort and he would be obliged to endure her snail-like pace. He was on the main road to the south and progressed quite well for a while, but it soon became obvious that the steadily falling snow was thickening and the wind rising. He would have to seek shelter before nightfall.

It was when he began to contemplate the possibility of reaching an inn and being snowed in for several days that a ghastly thought occurred to him. In a day or so his Mama would be travelling this very road and it would be just his luck to pick the sort of coaching inn where she, too, might seek shelter. He groaned. Imagine being snowed in for days and days with Demetria!

On impulse, therefore, he took the next left-hand turning, thinking that by so doing he might come across a smaller inn where he could lie up until the weather changed without the fear of hearing his mother's brittle, complaining voice as she crossed the threshold.

It was not a wise move. The snowstorm thickened, the road narrowed, and even Terror, Jerome's not ill-named stallion, showed signs of wishing that they might find shelter.

After half-an-hour of struggling, Jerome reined in and peered about him. A bleak moor stretched ahead, unblessed by human habitation, but just when he had begun to think he must turn back, he saw a movement ahead of him. Someone on horseback was slogging along through the storm and since, in such an out-of-the-way spot, it could scarcely be a stranger like himself, he spurred Terror to a trot, intending to overtake the other rider and get directions to the nearest shelter.

The distance between them narrowed, and the foremost rider glanced back. Then, to Jerome's astonishment, he dug his heels into his mount, lying low along its neck.

Jerome gave a shout, then spurred Terror into pursuit, and very soon he had overhauled the stranger until they were riding abreast. He called to the lad — for such it was — to stop, but the boy ignored him, and continued to ride flat out.

Thoroughly exasperated by such seemingly irrational behaviour, Jerome leaned over to grab the other's reins.

Then it happened. The rider dragged his horse's head round, the animal floundered towards the ditch, then slipped, falling onto its knees. And the rider flew through the air and crashed into the snow-covered hedge.

His mount, with a desperate heave, got itself back on its feet, took the hedge from a standing start in a way which, at any other time, would have earned Jerome's deepest admiration, and set off across the open moor as though the devil himself were on its tail.

CHAPTER
TWO

Vanessa felt herself going, clutched desperately at air, then landed with a muffled crash in the snow-filled ditch. Gasping and floundering, she struggled to her knees, her mind full of dread. Was it a highwayman? A murderer? Or just someone from Aunt Nessie, determined to drag her back to the safety of Bascombe Hall?

As she watched, the tall rider vaulted off his great black horse and came towards her. He came half into the ditch, remarking quite kindly, 'What on earth did you run away for? I only wanted to ask if you knew of an inn where I might shelter from the storm!' He chuckled and caught Vanessa beneath her armpits. 'I'm no highwayman, I promise you, so let's get you on your feet and see if you've broken any bones!'

It was unfortunate that his seeking hands caught Vanessa's most ticklish spot; she squeaked and wriggled sharply as he lifted her onto firm ground once more, then glanced into his face and surprised an odd expression in his eyes.

'I'm sorry ma'am, I thought you a . . . a . . .'

His voice faded into silence as his eyes travelled over her dishevelled figure. The cap which she had worn to hide her tumbling curls was still in the hedge, caught on a twig, and though her cloak was voluminous enough, beneath it he could not fail to see the boots and breeches which she had borrowed from her cousin Charlie's room.

Vanessa, in her turn, glanced up at her captor — and her gasp echoed the one he was giving. It was Jerome Harcourt, who had courted Pamela and insulted her own tender years!

But he did not know her. The eyes, travelling with dawning amusement over her apparel, did not show a flicker of recognition. Or not, at any rate, of her personality; it was her sex which brought the grin to his lips.

'I knew it! You're a girl, riding astride and dressed in breeches! But your hair . . .' his glance followed hers and he plucked the cap out of the hedge and handed it over to her with a sarcastic bow. 'Put it on, Viola!'

Her brows flew up? 'Viola? How . . .'

'Shakespeare, my dear little girl! Have you read *Twelfth Night*?'

She struggled out of his grasp, for he was still holding her steady, remarking acidly: 'Of course I have, and if I am to be that Viola, then I take it you're Malvolio?'

He followed her back onto the road, then began dusting the loose, powdery snow off her cloak. At her riposte one black brow was lazily raised but he only said pacifically, 'I've been called a fool, I take it, but I shan't repine. Poor Viola, to be discovered so soon! Well my dear, you're far too pretty to career round the country dressed as a boy for long, so you should be grateful to me for making the discovery sooner than later. I am, at least, gentleman enough not to take advantage of the situation.'

Vanessa was about to retort far from politely, when it occurred to her that only one horse stood patiently in the snowy road. She ran to the low hedge and peered into the whirling flakes which misted the moor, then turned, her eyes flashing dangerously. 'You stupid looby! Look what you've done! My h-horse has gone, with my saddlebags which contained all my wordly possessions. Don't just stand there, go after my horse at once, do you hear?'

'Go after him? He'll be miles away and I'm not risking Terror's legs by galloping across unknown, snow-covered terrain. And if I were you, Viola, I'd mind my manners! I'm the only means of getting you to shelter, me and Terror here. So button your lip!'

Vanessa ignored him, pushing through a thin place in the hedge and setting off at a stumbling run across the moor, calling wildly: 'Bullfinch! *Bullfinch!* Come back at once, you hen-hearted creature!'

There was no sound except for the moaning of the wind, then she heard muffled hoof-beats behind her and found herself snatched up in the air and thumped down, none too gently, on the crupper of the big, black stallion.

'You stupid, brainless female! What am I supposed to do if you break a leg out here? Or your, silly neck, come to that? Your horse is long gone! Now, I gather you're running away, so let me have the truth, if you please. What's your name, and where do you live? I intend to take you back to your parents as soon as I can, because they're probably half out of their minds with worry. Come along, no nonsense!'

The arm which held her was iron-hard and, suddenly, she felt very young and tired and far away from home. Remembering the full extent of her predicament brought tears to her eyes but she sniffed, and rubbed them away. Crying would not help!

'I don't h-have any parents, I live with an aunt. I've a guardian, a horrible old man who pays my aunt to live with me, because he cannot abide me. And I'd rather die than go back!'

'Fustian! But we'll leave that for the moment. Where were you bound, when your horse so abruptly shed you?'

'For my Godmama's house, in London. She invited me to spend the Season as her guest but my wretched guardian said I was not to go, so I ran away, of course.'

'Of course! And the name of your Godmama?'

She stiffened. 'What does it matter? I suppose you mean to cheat me and force me to return home? I won't go! I won't tell you my Godmama's name. I . . . I . . .'

Her voice faltered and sobs caught in her throat.

He shook her, but not unkindly. 'Stop that, no point in crying! I'll put you on the stage to London and pay for your ticket since I'm bound for the metropolis myself, and then I'll deliver you to your Godmama's house in person. But if you intend to trick me into leaving you alone in the city, I won't do it! I can tell from your voice that you're gently bred, and you've no idea what a dangerous city London can be. Now, are you going to tell me your Godmama's name and direction, or not'

'I'll tell you.' Her voice was subdued. 'She's Lady Harrison, married to Sir Everard, and they live in George Street.'

She twisted in his arm to look up into his eyes, the better to convince him of her sincerity, and saw the harsh lines of his face relax.

'Good girl! And your name? I give you my word that, unless circumstances alter drastically, I won't try to make you go home.'

She believed him, but something made her say shyly, 'Well, it's Viola Norris.'

He chuckled. 'No wonder you flew into a tantrum! And I am Jerome Harcourt. Well, Miss Norris, what I want to know is what will your godmother do when you turn up on her doorstep? After all, permission has been refused, and . . .'

For the first time, she smiled at him. 'It hasn't! That is to say, Lady Harrison won't know, because my guardian hates her and they don't speak. My guardian thinks *I've* written to refuse.'

Looking down at her, his dark eyes lit with an answering merriment. 'Oh Lord, you vixen! Well then, I'd best accompany you to London! I can see some buildings ahead and one of them looks like an inn. I hope it is, for I'm devilish hungry and half frozen with cold.'

It was an inn; as they drew level with it they could see the bright lamplight, the fireglow, and smoke issuing hospitably from the chimney.

'The Partridge Nest. Very suitable for two stormlings! Now, Miss Norris, you'd best be my young cousin and I think I'll call you . . . Oliver. Do you think you can answer to that?'

She nodded as he drew rein in the stableyard and lifted her down, then gave Terror's bridle to a skinny, bow-legged little ostler with instructions to groom the stallion, put a blanket over him, and then feed him hot mash and a judicious supply of oats.

The horse attended to, Jerome made for the inn, with Vanessa trotting after him. It proved to be a sizeable place, with a coffee room which boasted a log fire of immense proportions and a landlady who welcomed them with the information that she was even now roasting ducks for a party who had failed to turn up, doubtless due to

29

the inclement weather.

'Snow in March do be worse'n snow in January,' she remarked placidly, leading them across the hall. 'You'll be wanting a room, and I can let you 'ave the best bedchamber, for though we'm off the main road now, we get a power of travellers from time to time, so you'll find the bed aired, and I can light a fire quick enough.'

'Have you two rooms?' Jerome said, following the landlady's broad back up the stairs. 'My cousin talks in his sleep.'

'That I've not, sir, for we've two-three snow-bound travellers already, truth to tell. But if you'd rather, the lad could share wi' my son, in the attic.'

Jerome pretended to consider whilst Vanessa shot him a furious glance from beneath lowered brows.

'No, it's all right, I'll put cottonwool in my ears,' he said, grinning at his companion's scarlet face. The landlady opened a door and gestured them inside. Jerome glanced round perfunctorily, said 'Yes, quite suitable,' and requested water to wash and a light for the fire as quickly as possible.

Left alone with him Vanessa said breathlessly, 'A double bed! Well, you must sleep on the floor! I suppose I could go on, if the landlady would lend me a horse, but . . .'

'Rubbish, we'll just make the best of it.' Jerome was unpacking his bag and produced from its depths a hairbrush and some washing things.

'Here, brush your hair and I'll braid it for you. A queue is best for a stripling.'

He passed her the brush but after Vanessa had dabbed at her curls without much enthusiasm for a moment, he threw down his stock and seizing the brush, began to pull it through her hair with great force and little skill.

'Stop it, I can do it myself,' Vanessa ordered, her eyes watering with pain.

'Certainly not, I won't sit down to an over-cooked dinner just so a female can take three hours to do her hair, when three minutes will suffice! Stand still, young man, or I'll use this hairbrush on another part of your anatomy and you'll like that even less!'

Vanessa was about to answer hotly when she felt warning fingers grip her upper arm, and a voice from the doorway said: 'Please sirs, your 'ot water, and missus says dinner in twenty minutes.'

'Thank you. Oliver, stop wriggling,' Jerome said shortly.

Out of the corner of her eye, Vanessa could see a small, red-cheeked serving maid. The girl stood the jug of steaming water down on the washstand, gave Vanessa a sympathetic glance, and left the room, shutting the door quietly behind her.

'Lesson number one, always shut doors,' Jerome remarked. He finished braiding her hair, tied it with a black velvet ribbon, then turned her to face him, his eyes going critically over her

31

until the colour rose hot in her cheeks.

'Very neat,' he said approvingly, ignoring her embarrassment. 'Shall we dine?'

It was a good meal which they shared with three other men, two elderly farmers bound for market and now glad to seek the shelter of the inn overnight and a travelling doctor. Since none of their fellow guests seemed to have Jerome's uncanny knack of seeing through her disguise, Vanessa was able to enjoy her dinner and presently to enter with gusto into a game of backgammon with her benefactor.

Punch was called for and to make things more convincing, Jerome drank Vanessa's share as well as his own so that soon enough he was aglow with good spirits — though less in the sense that Vanessa assumed than in the literal sense!

They sat in the coffee room until the candles were guttering and the log fire was ashes, and then made their way up to their room. Here, Jerome threw off his coat, then shivered.

'Damme, but it's cold up here! I thought that woman was lighting a fire?'

'She did so, but we remained downstairs so long that it went out for lack of tending,' Vanessa said regretfully. 'Shall I go downstairs and fetch fresh logs and kindle it afresh?'

Jerome eyed the cold cinders distastefully.

'No, for you'd never find the log pile. Just get your coat and boots off and get into bed. You'll soon be asleep despite the cold. I suppose the bed was warmed earlier, when the fire was lit.'

'What are you going to do?' Vanessa asked suspiciously, glancing round the room. 'Sleep on that chair?'

Jerome had stripped back the covers and was arranging a bolster squarely down the middle of the bed.

'On that chair? No indeed, we'll share the bed. Don't worry, I shall respect the bolster, and keep to my own side!'

Vanessa eyed the chair doubtfully. It was very small and she did not fancy trying to sleep on it herself. She removed her coat and boots, then leapt into bed, pulling the covers up to her chin. Jerome removed his own boots and began to unbutton and remove his ruffled shirt. His chest was covered with dark, curly hair and she found her eyes drawn to it, half repelled, half fascinated.

Watching her, he said with amusement: 'It's all right, I don't expect you to follow my stoical example! This is the only shirt I've got with me and I don't want to crease it.'

'I shouldn't think you need a shirt, with all . . .' Vanessa felt her cheeks redden and shut her mouth firmly.

'With all this hair on my chest? How unkind you are, to make me feel unfairly favoured by fortune,' Jerome said smoothly. He climbed into bed and leaned across the bolster. 'Now say you're sorry for being rude by kissing me goodnight!'

'I wasn't rude and I won't kiss you! If you dare —'

'Damme, a challenge!'

Hard hands pulled her across the bolster, hard lips descended on her soft, amazed mouth. She tried to pull away but his arms were strong and she felt, as his mouth moved upon hers, a wild, mad desire to respond, to kiss him back. But it would be madness! She whimpered, pushing against his chest, and as suddenly as he had seized her he let her go.

'Too much hot punch,' he said, his voice lazily amused. 'Sorry, Viola! Now go to sleep because you're quite safe from me really; I've an aversion to red-heads. Goodnight, kitten.'

Before she could do more than gasp her outrage, he had turned over, snuggled beneath the covers and was breathing steadily, as if half asleep already.

Vanessa lay back, her heart still pounding, and wondered what to do for the best. Would she really be safe, or should she leave the room and try to woo sleep in the coffee room, downstairs? But the bed was blissfully warm already from their body-heat, the air icy. She imagined her toes touching the cold boards of the bedroom floor, the corridor, the stairs, of fumbling in the dark to find her coat and boots. She could not face it, and for the moment, at least, he seemed harmless enough. In fact, she should never have made that extremely personal remark about his hairy chest. Nor should she have almost dared him to kiss her. If she behaved sensibly and circumspectly, she was sure the rest of the night would pass without incident.

With a sigh, she curled right down into the covers, shoved her thumb in her mouth, and prepared to sleep.

But the thought kept going through her mind that she had got herself into an awful pickle. How shocked Aunt Nessie would be if she could see her now! How horrified dear cousin Rhoda! Her guardian and his wife would probably not show the least surprise. They would say they had always suspected that she was a hussy, and would demand that Jerome marry her, to save her good name.

That brought her thoughts up with a jerk. Poor Jerome, to be punished for his kindness! On the other hand, if he did try to take advantage of the situation she would tell him what his fate must be and that might dissuade him.

If she was forced to marry, she thought suddenly, who would really care whether she was happy or not? Her parents had died four years previously and she had spent a year with the Talbots, hating them, being as difficult as possible, homesick for Bascombe Hall, missing the warmth of her parents' love. Then Mr Talbot had conceived the bright idea of putting Aunt Nessie into the Hall as chatelaine and as a sort of substitute mother for his young charge. This had seemed wonderful at first to Vanessa. Aunt Nessie was so easy going, so anxious to please her niece. Vanessa had been growing fond of her aunt when she had discovered that Mr Frederick Talbot paid Aunt Nessie for bringing up the heiress.

After that, she had not gone out of her way to please Aunt Nessie nor to make friends with Rhoda and Charlie, her cousins. Why should she? They only wanted her because they needed her beautiful home and the money which she brought them. And then, lying rigidly on her half of the big bed, something else occurred to Vanessa. If her Godmama introduced her to the beau monde, she would still be no better off than before. She would never know whether men who flattered her, proposed marriage, pretended love, were more enamoured of her or her fortune!

It was too much. Abandoning all pretence of sleep Vanessa rolled over, buried her head in the pillow, and cried as if her heart would break.

When the bolster was removed she never even glanced up, being totally preoccupied with her grief. But when she was lifted out of her damp and soggy pillow, cradled in Jerome's arms, rocked and comforted, she did lift her head and take notice. Gasping and hiccuping, she began to tell him how no one loved her. She was a nuisance to her aunt, her cousins were bored by her, her guardian simply loathed her. She did not mention the disadvantages of her fortune, however, for that would have been vulgar. Instead she told him how even this escapade, which was to have been such fun, was turning sour on her.

'Why?' Jerome said gently, stroking the damp hair from her brow. 'You'll go to Lady Harrison's house and have a grand time, and then you'll marry a Duke, or a Prince, and live happily ever afterwards.'

'I don't wa-wan't to go to Godmama's house,' Vanessa wailed miserably. 'She only asked me to a-annoy my g-guardian! I wa-want to be with someone who wa-wants me!'

She clutched him convulsively, her small breasts beneath the fine linen shirt flattened against his chest so that he could feel the flutter of her heartbeat. He heard the steady thunder of his own heart quicken at her closeness, felt the supple softness of her against him, the scent of her hair giddying, for a moment, his senses.

Lightly, he kissed the side of her hot face, then moved his lips sensuously across her cheek, kissing her with small, half-teasing kisses until he reached her lips. This time, when their mouths met, he felt her tear-wet lips soften beneath his own, felt her melt against him, trusting him, comfortable with his caresses.

He knew, with a cold and still detached part of his mind, that she thought him a man of honour who could be kind to her in her distress and that this comforted her. Poor little unloved orphan, she believed him able to kiss and comfort her without wanting anything more because that was how she must be feeling. Yet how far from the truth this was, was becoming increasingly clear

37

to Jerome. She was all woman, breeches or no, and he must stop this whilst he still could.

He put her gently away from him, saying bracingly: 'Better? Then we'll try to get some sleep. If we get on the stage tomorrow, we've a long journey ahead of us.'

She moved away from him reluctantly, but already his comfort had relaxed her, brought her nearer sleep; her body curled up beneath the friendly warmth of clean sheets, her heavy eyelids drooped over her eyes.

But presently she said in a small voice, 'Jerome?'

He was wide awake now, intent on forgetting she was in the same bed, telling himself that she was at her most vulnerable, no more than an exhausted child, and that to take advantage of her would be a dog's trick.

'Mm hmm?'

'I thought you said you had an aversion to redheads?'

Despite himself, he chuckled.

'All cats are grey at night! Go to sleep, Viola!'

She wanted to ask him what he meant: cats were grey at night? What on earth did that have to do with his aversion for red-heads? But emotion and exhaustion were catching up with her. She opened her mouth to ask another question and fell into sleep like a stone falling into a well.

Jerome, regretting the remark as soon as it was made, took a deep breath and tried to prepare an explanation, then expelled it slowly as he heard her breathing deepen. Thank God, she was really asleep this time.

The bolster lay on the floor where he had thrown it. Should he get out of bed and put it back in position? It might be wiser. She was rather a sweet little thing when she wasn't being aggressive and tart. He sat up on one elbow and reached out to pluck the bolster from the floor but it was just out of reach. It was confoundedly cold out of bed! He sighed. Presently . . . presently . . .

And Jerome was asleep.

CHAPTER
THREE

Vanessa awoke to find her face resting against something warm, which stirred gently beneath her weight. She had no desire to wake up properly because she felt so happy, as though all her doubts and fears had dissolved during the night, never to re-form. Dimly, she could hear a steady thudding, and something was softly stirring her hair.

Opening one eye, she dreamily surveyed what appeared to be a small forest, quite close to her nose. It was heaving gently and she frowned, trying to remember what it reminded her of; a forest was not quite right, it was more like . . . like . . .

She moved her head to open both eyes and her heart gave a leap. She was curled up in Jerome Harcourt's arms, her cheek resting on his bare chest, one arm flung casually around him. The thudding she had heard was his heart-beat, and it was his breathing which had stirred her hair!

She remembered the bolster and frowned, momentarily puzzled by its evident disappearance. Then she remembered his comforting. I am dreadful, she thought without shame, an abandoned woman! But she could not unthink her contentment. A faint memory of last night's total misery and despair came back to her, and the manner in which Jerome had dispelled it. Had it really been like that? Had the sophisticated rake who had despised her so at Pamela's party really been so good and kind to her?

Cautiously, she moved her head until she was looking into Jerome's sleeping face. It was a face which would always be special for her now, awake or asleep. She studied the dark, thickly waving hair, the planes of his cheekbones, the halfmoons of thick, short eyelashes. She traced with her eyes the high-bridged, imperious nose, the clearly marked upper lip, the full lower one. Was it a sensuous mouth? She had no idea what a sensuous mouth was, but it sounded nice, so Jerome would have, for her, a sensuous mouth. She smiled to herself, knowing that it mattered not one jot. It was Jerome's mouth and, therefore, right.

I'm in love, Vanessa thought wonderingly. In love with a man I know to be a rake, because everyone said so at Pamela's party. He must be quite thirty, and therefore, incredibly experienced. And not only am I in love, her thoughts continued irrepressibly, but I have shared his bed!

This made her choke on a giggle, and immediately his heavy lids lifted and his eyes smiled lazily down at her, and his lips curved tenderly.

She smiled back, trembling, longing for his kisses, for whatever it was he had not done last night. She was somewhat hazy about the doings between men and women, but she was very sure he had behaved beautifully last night. She found herself wishing passionately that he would now cease to behave beautifully and love her, with kisses and caresses, and that mysterious something more which she was sure existed!

But after a moment of quiet contemplation his eyes widened and he sat up, tipping her off his chest.

'This won't do, Viola! It must be six o'clock, I should think, so we can get another couple of hours sleep before we need go down for breakfast. Go and see what the time is, there's a good little girl. My watch is on the dressing table.'

She slid off the bed and padded over to the dressing table.

'It is nearly six. Now can I come back to bed?'

He had plucked the bolster off the floor and had arranged it primly down the centre of the bed once more. He lay back, looking up at the ceiling. 'If you wish. What's the weather like?'

She peered out of the window, for the shutters had a gap of quite three inches between them.

'Still snowing.'

She padded back to the bed, jumped in, then,

after a quick, defiant glance, sent the bolster spinning across the floor. There, now he knew how she felt!

He glanced at her, his expression unreadable, then got out of bed, fetched the bolster, and replaced it. He said, in the tone of one humouring a small child: 'Now we mustn't get ideas! I really cannot make love to you in cold blood and in daylight, you know.'

The pain was so sharp that she felt the tears rush to her eyes, but they remained unshed. She saw him, dazzled with them, just a shape, but she had some pride left. She said steadily, with scarcely a quaver in her voice: 'Why are you so cross?'

The tears receded, leaving her eyes hot and dry, but she continued to eye him steadily.

'Because I very nearly made a fool of myself last night, my dear.' His voice was cool, even slightly amused. 'You're a cross-grained, red-headed minx, but last night I wanted you. I think it's greatly to my credit that you are as innocent this morning as you were when you went to bed last night!'

His words stabbed her to the heart. So she had meant no more to him than a woman's body in his bed, to be taken or not according, not to love or even lust, but to some strange male idea of honour!

'A-and this morning, you no longer w-want me? I'm glad!'

'That's a sensible girl. Now lie down, and we'll

43

sleep for a couple of hours, and when you wake up, you'll find all your romantical notions have gone and you'll be raring for London, and dances and parties!'

She could not answer for the tears which she was fighting to keep back. So he knew how she felt, had understood the message of desire implicit in the abandoning of the bolster! She felt as if she had bared her inmost soul to him and he had laughed it to scorn.

She huddled beneath the blankets, shivering, thinking to herself that unhappiness such as this made her brief woe of the previous night seem nothing. The pain of love given and not returned had to be experienced to be understood!

Presently, pride came to her aid. It was sheer foolishness, to imagine oneself in love with the first man who kissed one! He was very good looking, certainly, but she would meet men who were more handsome, men who were kinder, men who . . . She stopped, knowing that none of those things mattered, really. He might be just her first love, sweet but fleeting, but because of that brief moment when she had lain in his arms and smiled, and he had smiled back so tenderly, he would always be special. She told herself that she must be thankful that he had left her with her virtue intact, for she had an uneasy feeling that, had he possessed her, she would not have been able to dismiss him so lightly. It would be easier, she thought, when they were both in London. She would probably see him flirting with other women, women lovelier, wittier, more fashionable than herself. Then she would be able to despise him and turn to someone worthier. She was lucky that she had discovered the truth about him whilst her heart merely had a tiny crack in it, and was not broken from side to side!

She heard his breathing deepen, steady, then a tiny snore broke from him as he moved restlessly, pushing at the bolster. Vanessa curled her lip; sleeping already, like the hoggish creature he was! Well, it was morning, albeit early; she need no longer share either his bed or his room. Soon enough, someone would be up downstairs, lighting fires, boiling kettles, making cups of hot chocolate and light scones with farm butter spread thickly. She would dress now, and leave him where he was, to snore undisturbed by her presence or her "romantical notions".

She crept across the cold floor, found her boots, and sat down to tug them on. Her coat was over the chair, she would slip that round her shoulders, and carry her stock.

She crossed to the chair, picked up her coat and stock, then glanced towards the shutters. Good, there was movement outside already, so someone was already up and about. Or could it have been just the lazily drifting snowflakes?

She crossed to the window and looked out into the stable yard. Sure enough, a man was crossing it, leading a pony. She could see him and the animal quite distinctly and suddenly she peered even more closely, her heart giving a joyous leap. Was it? Could it be . . . ? The man swung the pony sideways to her, opening the stable door, and she knew she was right. It was Bullfinch, her own mount!

She turned from the window as Jerome stirred sleepily in the bed. She froze where she was, but he did not open his eyes, he only pulled the blankets over his exposed shoulder.

On tiptoe, Vanessa made for the door, opened it almost noiselessly, and was about to leave the room when a voice from the bed said: 'Where are you going?'

Vanessa jumped, then said coldly, 'Out.'

'Not out in the snow, I trust? I shan't pay your shot or get you a ticket on the stage if you do anything foolish!'

Vanessa gritted her teeth, but bit back a desire to tell him to mind his own business.

'I'm going down to have a warm by the fire, and to see if I can procure a cup of hot tea or chocolate or something.'

He grunted. 'Very well. Tell the chambermaid to wake me up no later than eight.'

She vouchsafed no reply, leaving the room and shutting the door softly behind her, but she had no intention whatsoever of passing on his message! Let him lie in bed till noon, she would tell the landlady. He's had a disturbed night, and needs to have his sleep out! For she intended to have a good breakfast and then take Bullfinch and make her way to London as she had planned! She would not wait to be humiliated by Jerome Harcourt, when, by riding ahead ten miles or so, she might reach London without his aid!

Jerome woke late and bad tempered, to find sunlight streaming in through the gap in the shutters and sounds of bustle in the room below making it obvious that he had overslept.

He rolled out of bed, cursing the punch, which had undoubtedly caused his head to feel as if someone were trying to wrench it off, and reached for his clothes. He glared balefully towards the door. Women! He had told that chit to see he was woken at eight, but had she obeyed him? Forgotten all about him, no doubt, in the bustle and excitement of an inn. He buttoned his shirt, tied his stock, and dragged his coat on anyhow, a deep scowl still marring his forehead. Damn *all* women! He had hurt her feelings, of course he had, it was the only way out of what had nearly turned out to be a seduction scene — though who had been seducing whom he would not have cared to hazard a guess!

His boots were still mired from the night before and he swore again, remembering that in his haste to get into bed he had forgotten to stand them outside the door for cleaning. He must have been drunk last night! When he thought, now, what the consequences of his comforting Viola might have been, he turned cold. She was gently bred, that was obvious

47

from the first moment she opened her mouth. Though patently of little importance, with a name completely unknown to him, he had no doubt that she had relatives who were quite capable of calling him to account had he taken advantage of her position. And it would be difficult, if not impossible, to persuade anyone that Jerome Harcourt had taken a woman into his bed and not seduced her!

He brushed his hair, rubbed his face vigorously with his flannel, dried it, and then made for the door. He would give young Viola a piece of his mind, letting him oversleep like that!

Downstairs, the coffee room was warm, the smell of breakfast inviting. The landlady hurried forward, setting a bowl of kedgeree on the table, promising him bacon and eggs in no time at all. He ordered coffee, then asked, after a quick glance round to ascertain that Viola was not sulking in a corner somewhere, where his cousin had gone.

'I don't know I'm sure, sir,' the landlady said placidly. 'For a bit of a walk, per'aps? It isn't snowing, and the sun's shining.'

'A walk? Where could he walk to?' Jerome asked, frowning. 'I hope he hasn't got himself into any mischief.'

At the back of his mind a vague fear was forming. Had his words been too effective? He had meant to warn her away from falling in love with him, not to send her rushing off in weather like this!

The landlady clapped a hand to her forehead.

'Bless me, sir, I'll forget my own name next! The young gennelman left a note!'

Jerome's heart sank as he took the folded sheet of paper. It was quite brief and to the point.

'*Have gone ahead,*' it said. '*Don't come after me. I shall be quite all right.*'

He glanced up from the page to find the landlady still regarding him placidly.

'My cousin says he's gone ahead. Surely not on foot?'

'I'll find out for you, sir.'

He poured himself a coffee and then drank it so hot that he burnt his mouth. Something else to put down to Viola's account, he told himself. Wretched girl, so this was how she repaid his kindness. He tried to forget what he had said to her, how cruelly he must have wounded her self-esteem.

'The stable lad says he rode out quite early, sir. And he's not returned.'

That was the landlady, returning soft-footed from her errand.

Jerome jumped to his feet with an oath, over-turning the coffee pot and ruining the landlady's best lace-trimmed tablecloth.

'Rode? My God, he'll be killed! Terror's no mount for a g— for a stripling!'

He cast his napkin down, shouted over his shoulder, 'Have my bill ready in five minutes!' and went straight to the stable.

To his amazement, Terror regarded him over

the halfdoor whilst the stable lad, a skinny, tow-headed youth of fifteen or sixteen, continued to groom the big horse.

'Where's my cousin? When did he get back?'

The lad straightened, regarding this elegant but possibly insane gentleman with caution.

'Back, sir? He ain't back, your honour. Gone long since, as I told missus.'

A jerk of the head indicated the landlady.

'But your mistress said my cousin rode out! Did you hire him a horse? He had no money, and I certainly don't intend to pay for him to break his neck!'

'Oh, he din't tell ye, then?' Light dawned on the lad's unprepossessing countenance. 'Farmer Stott found a rat-tailed grey, wanderin' on the moor near his farmhouse. He brung him in this mornin', for to see if anyone knewed who he belonged to. And the young gennelman knewed 'im at once. I see'd you both ride in on the stallion 'ere, so I knewed the young gennelman must have lorst his mount.'

'His own *horse?* It came back? With the saddlebags untampered with, of course.' Jerome frowned, gazing at Terror but not seeing him. Instead, he saw a pair of tear-bright green eyes and a tumbled mass of red-gold curls. What would she do? Make for London on horseback, in this weather? To be sure it was no longer actually snowing and the sun shone, but he would not be at all surprised to find it snowing again, or at least bitterly cold, once the sun had set.

50

He stood there for a moment, sightlessly staring at the horse, then swung on his heel and returned to the inn. He packed quickly, paid his shot and left, his breakfast unconsumed and congealing upon the coffee-room table.

The stable lad, rightly guessing his intentions, had saddled and bridled Terror and at the very moment that Jerome stepped into the yard had brought the stallion out. Jerome mounted, threw the lad a half-guinea which brought an enormous grin to the boy's face, and turned Terror out onto the road. He hesitated there, then wheeled the horse round to call back to the lad: 'Did you see which way she went?'

'Forrard, your honour, towards the pike,' the boy replied, gesturing up the road. He watched Terror and his rider disappear into the distance then returned to his own work, muttering under his breath: 'though the lad was riding a gelding, not a mare!'

Meanwhile Vanessa, riding along with Bullfinch between her knees and the comfortable knowledge that her money, her feminine apparel, and her toilet things were safely stowed in the saddlebags on either side of her, where they had been all along, should have felt perfectly content. Certainly she feared no pursuit, for Jerome had made his feelings plain; he had felt sorry for her plight but now that she had her horse and her belongings, he would be glad enough to see the back of her. Unfortunately, however, content-

51

ment seemed to have no place in this snowy, sunny landscape, all she could summon up was a dreary satisfaction that at least she was her own mistress now, and no burden to anyone. Armed with her aunt's money, she intended to ride to the nearest coaching inn on the main turnpike to London, change back into her gowns and bonnets, and take her place in the coach. It was a shame that she could not ride to London on Bullfinch, but in weather such as this it was out of the question. She would leave Bullfinch at the inn to be called for, and write a letter to Aunt Nessie, telling her of the pony's whereabouts. She would also repay Mr Harcourt any monies he had laid out on her behalf.

Presently, the side road she was on joined the main turnpike road and she guessed that, probably no more than half-a-dozen miles ahead, she would find a sizeable coaching inn where she might await the stage. But now that she thought about it, she realised that to catch the stage today would almost certainly mean an awkward and embarrassing journey in Jerome's company. She drew rein, considering what best to do. There could be little doubt that, when she reached the nearest coaching inn, she would find Jerome joining her in good time for the stage.

Ignoring the little flutter of pleasure that she felt at such a prospect, she cast her mind about for some alternative, and presently remembered that the farmer who had returned Bullfinch to the inn that morning had told her his next port of call would have been the coaching inn and after that, the village of Brunwell, where there was a nice little inn where the quality sometimes put up for a night or two.

Closing her eyes, she conjured up a picture of the jovial, red-faced farmer. When he had been talking to her, he had gestured to the right, as if to indicate. . . .

A turning, off to the right, seemed like a sign. She turned Bullfinch into it, praying that she would find a village, and after a couple of uneventful miles the first cottages began to appear.

Brunwell, it seemed, was a large village, or perhaps even a very small town. Jogging along, Vanessa saw a baker's shop, a butcher's shop, a blacksmith's forge and a small draper's shop with a window for millinery. Further along the street, a swinging sign announced the Falcon Inn, which seemed pleasant enough.

Vanessa rode into the stable yard, handed Bullfinch's reins to a groom, and made, with what self-confidence she possessed, for the coffee room. Despite the sunshine it was cold outside, and she was not sorry to enter the warmth, to call for a pot of coffee, and to sit down beside the log fire.

She was sitting there, gazing at the flames and sipping her coffee, wondering when she should ask for a room, when a commotion outside announced the arrival of more visitors. Even as she wondered, half hopefully, whether Jerome had woken up and come in search of her, the door to the coffee room was flung open and a young woman entered, saying over her shoulder to someone in the hall, 'Take her to a room at once, if you please, and send for the doctor! I cannot abide her moanings and groanings a moment longer!'

Vanessa stared, then shot to her feet.

'Matty! What in heaven's name are you doing here?'

The young woman turned and gazed incredulously at Vanessa, taking in her youth's clothing, her mired boots and her cheeks flushed from the fire. She was a pretty young woman, handsomely dressed in strawberry pink velvet with a charming, shallow-crowned hat perched on her yellow curls, and with diamond eardrops in her ears, a cherry-coloured cloak with a taffeta lining flung back carelessly over her shoulders, and an indefinable aura of wealth and self confidence about her.

'Van? Can it really be you? Dear me, what a terrible creature you are! What start is this? Breeches! My Papa would have a fit if he could see you now, despite his high opinion of you!'

Vanessa hurled herself into her friend's arms.

'Oh, Matty, what a wonderful piece of luck to find you here, in this tiny place! But what can you be doing? I've run away from Aunt Nessie and was on my way to London when I was caught in a snowstorm. And you?'

The blonde beauty had been in the act of shedding her cloak; she now completed her task,

54

looking round impatiently for a servant to take it and then, with a shrug, folding it over the back of the settle and sitting down opposite Vanessa.

'My dear girl! Running away! Not but what I'm in some sort of a pickle myself. My wretched coach overturned on a slippery corner and my abigail, Mercy, was thrown out of the door and into the ditch. You have never heard such a fuss! Screams, faints, vapours, and I am perfectly sure she's un-hurt. I very much hope she is at any rate, since I'm on my way to London, and since I'm expected I can't remain at this inn for days and days!'

'On your way to London! Oh, Matty, may I not accompany you? I am to visit my Godmama, who lives in George Street.'

Matty got to her feet and tugged impatiently at the bell-pull.

'What a shatterbrain you are, Vanessa, you were always the same at school! Tell me your story from the beginning; how you came to run away, why you are in boy's breeches, and . . . oh, everything! As for accompanying me to London, that's all very fine, but my coach will be days and days repairing, and one of the horses broke a leg and had to be despatched. As it is, I should hire a coach, but if Mercy really is as ill as she sup-poses, how can I persuade her to chaperon me to my Godfather's house? For . . .'

'I can!'

The fashionable young lady stared at the flushed stripling.

'You!'

'Of course, Matty; why not? I've gowns and petticoats and things in my saddle bags and I was going to catch the stage! If we are together, all is instantly respectable.'

'Oh, but . . . no, I won't listen to you, Van, until you tell me the whole story.' At this point a maid answered the bell by popping her head round the door and grinning enquiringly at them. 'You, girl, fetch me a tray of chocolate and some sweet biscuits.'

The girl bobbed a curtsy and disappeared and Vanessa, with a sigh, began on the saga of her decision to run away to London. But although the two girls had been close friends at the select seminary they had attended for two years, she did not feel it wise to mention Jerome other than as a friendly traveller who had shared her dinner at the inn the previous night, and offered to see her safely onto the London stage.

When she finished the story and sat back, Matty eyed her thoughtfully, head on one side.

'Yes. I do see you had a good reason for running away, though . . . but never mind, you've done it now. I see no reason why we can't continue our journey together, especially as I'm sure that Mercy will insist upon lying here for days together. She's not a young woman, and she's had an epidemic cold for two or three days, which is probably why she showed so little spirit when the coach overturned.'

'Oh, good! And Matty, how am I to be turned back into a girl again, for assuredly your maid won't see you go off to London in a hired coach with a lad for company!'

Matty considered, narrowing her eyes and gazing at her companion.

'I've only just arrived, so no one knows what my party consists of. Vanessa, you must go out to the stable and take your clothing up to the loft. Change, then wait there for me.'

'It's awfully cold outside,' Vanessa said doubtfully. 'Don't be long, will you, or I'll most probably freeze to death.'

Matty pushed her out impatiently.

'Of course I won't be long. Just do as I say!'

In the event, it proved a far simpler matter than either girl had anticipated. Vanessa slipped out to the stables, to find them in a ferment with four extra horses, the two outriders bustling here and there, a coachman and a guard who seemed to be nursing an injured shoulder.

She slipped amongst them without anyone giving her more than a glance, climbed quietly up into the loft, changed into a pale green gown, and waited.

Very soon, she heard the tap-boy come across the cobbles and announce loudly, 'The lady says as 'ow she'll give ye all a tot of rum before any more work is done, if ye do but hurry into the taproom.'

Vanessa could not help chuckling as the stable emptied as if by magic and, presently, a voice called softly, 'Vanessa?'

'Here I am!'

Vanessa slithered quickly down the ladder and stood smiling at her friend.

'Good! You look quite respectable now, except for your hair. I've brought a brush and some ribbons.'

A few moments were sufficient to banish Oliver for ever, and to bring Miss Vanessa Bascombe into her own again. But neither young woman wasted time on self-congratulation.

'Come along, back to the inn, then I'll bid poor Mercy a fond farewell and we'll hire a conveyance to get us back onto the pike road.'

That was Matty, seizing her friend's hand. But Vanessa hung back, giving an exclamation of dismay.

'Oh, no! Look, Matty!'

Outside, the sky was grey and already snow whirled, thick and white, making it difficult to see the short distance across the courtyard to where the inn waited to welcome them. Further travel that day was plainly impossible.

CHAPTER FOUR

It was dark before Jerome arrived at the Falcon, and by the time he did so, there was murder in his heart. That wretched chit of a girl! He had ridden straight to the coaching inn, to find no trace of either his cousin Oliver or the rat-tailed grey she had ridden. On he went, having decided that she must have wanted to avoid him and so had gone to the next inn where the London stage would stop. There had been no such visitor that day, the landlord assured him. Nor had there been a young lady such as he described. And it was the look which accompanied that last remark which had brought Jerome out of the inn again, black-browed, determined not to wait there for the London stage!

By then, anyway, he was sufficiently worried about the goose of a girl to be determined to run her to earth. He tortured himself with hideous visions of seduction and rape, of the innocent trust she had placed in him being grossly misplaced by another, of her running into the storm without a penny piece or a coat . . . For the first time in his life, Jerome knew complete and total anxiety for a person he now knew had been in his charge. It was all very well to tell himself that she was just a foolish little runaway and no business of his! He had made her his business by taking her into his charge the previous night, had even, perhaps, made her more vulnerable by behaving honourably towards her. And now he must find her, he must!

As soon as he stabled Terror, he knew his search was at an end. The stable was full of mounts, but the rat-tailed grey who rolled an en-quiring eye from the next stall could be no other than the fleet-footed Bullfinch.

Jerome hastened across the stableyard as soon as Terror was groomed and fed, crashed open the door of the coffee room, and strode in. There was only one other occupant of the room, a slender girl in a green gown with reddish-gold curls piled high on her head. She raised a startled face at his entry, and he saw the colour drain from her cheeks, leaving her paper-white.

'You! Running away, leaving me stupid notes, frightening the life out of me . . . By God, if I ever had the schooling of you I'd beat you till you couldn't sit down! And what on earth are you doing in petticoats, you brainless creature? How can I escort you on the stage in such a state, without you bidding your reputation goodbye?' He seized her arm, jerking her to her feet. 'Who

60

are you with? Is it a man? Has anyone offered you insult? I'll break every bone in his body!'

He was gripping her upper arms, lifting her half off her feet, and he noticed for the first time that the green eyes had flecks of gold in them, and that her pupils were ringed with a darker shade of green.

'Jerome, don't!' He knew she was frightened by his sudden appearance and shook her again, wanting to punish her for the anxiety she had caused him. 'I'm all right! In fact, I'm here with a friend. Do put me down before someone comes in!'

She was regaining her colour now, a faint, sweet pink stained her cheeks and her mouth drooped, soft and red, showing her small white teeth. For one crazy moment he longed to take her in his arms, to crush her mouth with his, to feel her begin to yield to him. Then he stood her down and pushed her away from him, even as he saw a sparkle of annoyance replace the fright in those big green eyes.

'Jerome, how dare you? Have you run mad? You've no right to treat me so! And you may leave the inn this instant, for I'm very sure there's no room!'

'I intend to, and I'm taking you with me! Where is your cloak?'

She smiled at him, imps of wickedness lurking in her eyes. She also sat down again.

'I'm not going with you, I'm staying here with my friend Matty.'

Jerome snorted. 'Matty! A likely story! Viola, I'm ashamed of my behaviour last night, but I was intoxicated, if you want the truth, and like it or not, I'm responsible for getting you to London safely, and without a slur on your character. Now put your things into a bag, there's a good girl, and we'll try to get back to the coaching inn. I've a room there, and . . .'

Vanessa was shaking her head, a smile playing about her lips.

'We wouldn't get back to the coaching inn, not unless the weather has improved drastically since I last looked outside. I daresay it was all Terror could do to get you this far, and he's much bigger and stronger than Bullfinch! And my friend is not a figment of my imagination, but a very dear person who has promised to take me to London with her when the weather clears. So you may be easy. Indeed, if you wish to stay here the night I'll introduce you to her in the morning. She's gone to bed now, but will be up betimes, hoping for a change in the weather.'

He was conscious of a ludicrous feeling of disappointment as his belief in her friend's existence was strengthened by her words. So there really was a friend! But even so, he could not leave her here with some slip of a girl, some farmer's daughter, probably, by the sound of her name.

'I'll stay the night,' he decided. 'After all, it's four miles back to the coaching inn and I'm tired. But I really think you ought to set out with me tomorrow, Viola. I'm in a hurry to get to the metropolis for I'm expected, and . . .'

She interrupted him, a guilty twinkle in her eye. 'Oh, dear! My name isn't Viola, it's Vanessa! I have to tell you, because otherwise poor Matty would give me away accidentally. And she, too, is in a hurry to reach the city, so as soon as the weather clears we shall set off ourselves.'

'Vanessa!' He shrugged, throwing his overcoat over the back of a chair and sinking into its cushioned comfort. 'By God, I'm worn out. Tell me how you came to meet this girl and where you knew each other previously?'

Vanessa perched on the edge of the chair and spoke quickly.

'We met at school in Harrogate, and Matty's here because her abigail broke a leg when the coach overturned, so they came into the nearest inn to shelter.' She chuckled suddenly. 'You would have been quite shocked at the indifference with which Miss Randolph regards her dependant or pretends to! But when she found out poor Mercy had really broken her leg she was so sweet, and insists that we stay until the woman feels more the thing. I wonder if she would have been so generous had we not been snowed in!'

Jerome sighed. 'An abigail with a broken leg? What next must happen to try my patience? First, you lose your horse and . . .' he broke off, glancing at her, his gaze suddenly intent. 'Miss *Randolph?*'

'That's right. Matty is really Miss Mathilda Randolph. Why? Don't say you know her, Jerome?'

He glanced down at his boots, absently rubbing the melting snow off them with one long, tanned finger.

'I believe she may be the young lady who is to stay in Hanover Square with my uncle, Sir Thomas Remington. If it's true, what an odd coincidence! But why are you getting up? Surely you're not rushing upstairs to bed already?'

Vanessa, who was on her feet and halfway to the door, sighed.

'Think, dear Jerome! If there is no room for you here, the least I can do is to suggest to the landlady that I share either Matty's accommodation or Mercy's! I think I had best sleep in Mercy's room actually, because she may need some attention in the night. And in any event, I must go to Mathilda now, because she is making Mercy comfortable and may need me. Goodnight, sir.'

Jerome had risen to his feet and bowed.

'Goodnight, ma'am. I take it I shall see you at breakfast?'

Vanessa giggled. 'Perhaps! I take it that the landlady gave you my note?'

'I shall endeavour to forget your foolish and thoughtless behaviour of the past hours,' Jerome said icily. 'Perhaps then we may deal better together.'

'I shall also endeavour to forget yours,'

Vanessa reminded him gently. 'For you no longer need to worry over me, sir, if you ever did! I have my friend to take care of me and to chaperon me as necessary. I need no other!'

She was about to whisk through the door when Jerome, driven by curiosity said: 'Is Miss Randolph older than you, Viola? Or the same age?'

'She's just eighteen. But because of her upbringing and circumstances, she is a great deal more able to take care of herself than I! She will have nothing to fear from you! Goodnight, sir!'

She was out of the door and shutting it behind her before he could think of a suitable retort.

Rather to Vanessa's surprise, Mathilda greeted the information that a young man was staying at the inn with considerable interest. When Vanessa told her that Jerome had arrived the previous evening, and would be introduced to her at breakfast, her whole demeanour underwent an abrupt change. She had been sitting at the dressing table, rather sulkily combing her hair into ringlets, but she threw down the comb and reached for a swansdown puff, plying it vigorously on her nose.

'A man? How exciting! How came you to meet him, Van? Is he handsome? Dark or fair? Well, at least he will be another face to look at, over breakfast!'

'He's dark and quite good looking, I suppose,' Vanessa said cautiously. 'I told you I'd met a man who befriended me earlier. It's him. He followed me here, thinking I might be in some sort of trouble. The only thing is, he believes my name to be Vanessa Norris, and I would rather you didn't tell him the truth.'

Mathilda reached for a patch and stuck it in the middle of one cheek, then pulled it off again with a grimace.

'That doesn't become me! Why don't you want him to know your name?' Through the mirror, her china-blue eyes widened as they fixed on her friend's face. 'Oh Van, don't say he's a fortune hunter! My papa went on and on about the horrid creatures until he quite frightened me!'

'No, he's very respectable, he's Sir Thomas Remington's nephew,' Vanessa said reassuringly. 'I don't want him sending any messages to Aunt Nessie about me until I'm safe with my Godmama, that's all, so I shan't tell him my real name.'

'Oh, I see.' Mathilda picked up a pearl necklace and fastened it round her neck. 'All right, I won't tell. How does this necklace look with this gown?'

'Pearls? At this hour of the day? No, don't take them off, you goose, I was only teasing! I've no idea what the best people wear to eat ham and eggs in!'

Laughing and reminiscing over their days at school the two girls went downstairs and into the coffee room. Jerome already sat at the table in the window, and jumped to his feet, pulling out a chair.

'Come and sit down, both of you,' he ordered. 'Miss Norris, you must introduce me to your companion.'

He gave Mathilda a charming smile, then, as the introductions were rather ungraciously performed by Vanessa added, 'But since I asked Miss Norris last night whether you were bound for Sir Thomas Remington's house, I feel I know you already! I am Sir Thomas's nephew, so this unexpected meeting merely means we shall get to know one another a few days sooner than we should otherwise have done.'

'Why?' Vanessa said baldly. 'I thought you were determined to get to London as soon as possible.'

Jerome smiled slightly.

'Yes, indeed! But since the weather plainly forbids any journeying, I must admit I look forward to sharing my incarceration with two such fair companions.'

The remark was addressed, ostensibly, to them both, but the glance from beneath his heavy lids was directed at Mathilda alone.

He's flirting with her, Vanessa thought, considerably put out. Why should he flirt with Mathilda, a young woman he had met scarcely two minutes earlier? To be sure, she was picture-book pretty, with her golden ringlets, milky skin and big, pale blue eyes, but surely he could not have so rapidly formed an attachment?

It seemed he could. Though he made no more overt efforts to attract her interest, Vanessa soon realised that this was because her friend's attention was well and truly caught. She was like a moth fluttering round a lamp, unable to make a remark without glancing over to see how Jerome had taken it, talking in an artificial manner with much laughter, cries of 'La, sir!' and what Vanessa decided must be 'roguish glances', though she had never actually seen a roguish glance until that day.

Outside, it continued to snow steadily. It was impossible to go out even for a short walk and the landlady was beginning to mutter about her food supply and her cellar.

Darkness fell, and the three of them played spillikins, a childish game which Vanessa enjoyed though Mathilda yawned over it, pretending that it was far beneath her.

At length, after what seemed to Vanessa to have been the longest day of her life, the girls made their way up to their rooms, leaving Jerome yawning over a book by the fire. But as soon as Vanessa had seen Mercy comfortably sleeping, she pulled on her cloak and tiptoed down to the coffee room.

Jerome looked up as she came in, his glance brightly expectant, then got to his feet, saying: 'What's this? Where's Miss Randolph? You're a messenger, I suppose?'

'No I am not!' Vanessa said tartly. She crossed to the fire and threw herself into the chair opposite the one he had just vacated. 'I came to ask you what on earth you're doing to my poor friend? She seems to have lost her senses!'

Jerome sat down opposite her, crossed his legs, and regarded her beneath lowered lids.

'She's a pretty little creature, and she's not known many men. She rather likes me!'

'Well, she wouldn't if she knew . . .'

'Do you intend to tell her?'

Vanessa flushed. 'Of course not; there's nothing to tell, after all. But you certainly did not encourage me to behave in such a . . . a wanton fashion!'

He raised black brows, a faint smile hovering on his lips.

'My dear child, you know *nothing!* Miss Randolph and I are indulging in a little light flirtation. Never fear that I shall step beyond the line of what is proper, for I shall do no such thing. And now be off to bed or it is *you* who will get talked about and not Miss Randolph.'

Vanessa pursed her lips. 'Well, just remember, I know you a great deal better than my friend does, and I don't intend to see her made a fool of, as I was.'

She was at the door, and curtsyed mockingly, her bright smile suddenly lighting up her face.

'Goodnight, dear Jerome! Sweet dreams!'

'Wait, Vanessa, I . . .'

But she ignored his outstretched hand, shutting the door firmly upon him and running lightly up the stairs and back to the room she was

69

sharing with Mercy. The abigail was awake again, thirsty, peevish and uncomfortable. As she rang for a cool drink for the woman, re-arranged the contraption which kept the blankets off Mercy's leg, and poured the draught the doctor had left into a medicine glass, Vanessa reflected that she would not be sorry when the snow cleared and enabled them to continue their journey to the metropolis. Even at school, Mathilda Randolph had been extraordinarily clever at getting other people to do all the work, and it was obvious that the gift had not failed her as she grew older!

She climbed into her own bed at last, and blew out the big candle, so that only the small light on the mantelpiece illuminated the room. Snuggling down, she reflected that it was probably foolish of her to worry over Mathilda. The older girl had a doting father and a great many relatives to advise her and generally see that no harm came to her.

But I, in effect, introduced her to Jerome, Vanessa remembered uneasily. And however drunk he may have been, I *know* him to be a rake, and unprincipled! Suppose he has . . . has *designs* on poor Matty?

She struggled to think of a solution to her problem for a while but she really was tired after her long and boring day, and her lids would droop despite herself. Just before she fell asleep it did occur to her that it was Matty who was doing most of the chasing at present, but she also realised that Jerome was far too clever — and too experienced — to openly pursue a quarry.

It also occurred to her that Jerome must know that Matty Randolph was a considerable heiress, and it was this attribute which had suddenly roused his interest in her friend. But she was ashamed of the thought, banished it immediately. He was a number of nasty things, a rake, perhaps a libertine, certainly selfish and single-minded, but that did not make him a fortune hunter!

'Well, Miss? What's the weather doing this morning, then? Mercy, sitting up in bed with her nightcap askew and a cup of hot milk on the table beside the bed, looked more cheerful for a good night's sleep and was obviously feeling a great deal better.

Vanessa, dressed and brushing out her hair, moved to the shutters and drew them right back.

'The snow's stopped, thank goodness, and the sun's shining,' she reported. 'The doctor doesn't want you moved, Mercy, but if the snow thaws, I daresay Miss Mathilda will want to continue her journey today.'

Mercy reached for the hot milk and sipped with noisy enjoyment.

'First thing I've fancied, this milk,' she stated. 'As to Miss Matty leaving, I've no doubt she'll do so. But she'll see I'm taken care of, for her Pa would give it her hot and strong if she did otherwise.'

'I'm sure her own conscience wouldn't let her just abandon you,' Vanessa protested. 'She's not an *unkind* girl, Mercy!'

'No,' Mercy agreed reflectively. 'Just thoughtless, and selfish. Her Pa's a good man, but he gives her her own way too much. Still, she'll learn.'

'Yes. Well, with the sun shining and no snow actually falling, I shall go out for a walk,' Vanessa decided. 'I'll send you up a tray of breakfast, Mercy. Is there anything else I can do for you?'

'Ooh Miss, is there such a thing as a book in the place? Mercy asked rather surprisingly. 'I do like a good read, but being as how Miss keeps me busy, I don't often get the chance. Now, lying here with nothing to do but think, I've fair *craved* something to read!'

'I'll try and find you something. A novel, perhaps?'

'Yes please, Miss,' Mercy said eagerly. 'Something real exciting, like *The Castle of Otranto*! Ooh, my blood ran cold when I read a bit of that!'

'There's bound to be *something*,' Vanessa said hopefully. 'I won't forget, Mercy.'

But upon enquiring of Mathilda, when they met over breakfast, she learned that her friend had not so much as glanced at a book since leaving school two years earlier.

'Not even a novel?' Vanessa enquired, spreading orange marmalade on a crumbly scone and biting into it.

'Not even a novel,' Mathilda confirmed. 'Reading is a waste of time! And you may be surprised to learn that I usually have my breakfast in my room, on a tray!'

'Usually, you've an abigail to serve it and a cook to prepare it,' Vanessa reminded her. 'Here, there's only poor Mrs Lubbock, the landlady, to cook for us all, and Rosie to serve everyone. In fact, when I saw Rosie earlier, she said the bootboy hadn't come up from the village, so they're short-handed as well.'

'Hmm. I wonder when Jerome will be down?'

'Mathilda! You should call him Mr Harcourt, you know you should!'

Mathilda was in blue today; she looked very pretty and very wilful, and the glance she shot at her friend was full of naughtiness.

'Why? You called him Jerome twice last evening!'

'I did? Oh dear, well that was because when we first met I was in breeches and he called *me* Oliver, so naturally I called him Jerome, as he bade me. Old habits die hard!'

Mathilda poured herself coffee, sipped it, then added in a nonchalant tone; 'I asked him to call me Mathilda, as it happens. After all, we're practically *related!* His uncle is my Godfather!'

'I can't very well object to his using my given name, since I infinitely prefer that to Miss Norris! Mathilda, I do advise you never to start telling small lies, because they're apt to lead to so much confusion. I really rather wish I'd told

Jerome my real name from the start.'

Mathilda pursed her lips and nodded emphatically, at the same time dusting her hands together and rising to her feet.

'You're quite right, Van. And now, should we send the chambermaid to rouse Jerome? There may be a possibility that the stage could arrive today since it is thawing.'

At this moment the door opened and Jerome walked in, shivering and holding out his hands to the heartening blaze on the hearth.

'Good morning, young ladies! I was up hours since, seeing to the horses, and though it really is thawing, the outside world is no place for two gently nurtured girls, I can promise you. It is cold, and extremely wet underfoot, and no coachman in his senses would drive anyone anywhere, unless it was a matter of life and death!'

'Well, I'm going out,' Vanessa declared. 'And what's this about the stage, Matty? I thought you had quite decided to hire us a coach?'

Mathilda shrugged, glancing at Jerome through her thick, fair eyelashes.

'Well, I thought that if Mr Harcourt was going on the stage, we might as well do the same. After all, it will make the journey far less tiresome if we're together.'

'Not at all. I insist that I hire a coach and see you young ladies safe to Hanover Square!'

'Or, in my case, to George Street,' Vanessa said crossly. 'Really, you two, you're being quite absurd. We're going to meet often enough in

74

London I daresay, without living in each other's pockets in a coach! And if the snow really does clear, surely you'll ride Terror the rest of the way, Mr Harcourt?'

Jerome turned his dark eyes on her, the expression in them one of infuriating mockery.

'And leave you to travel unescorted? What a wretch you must think me, Miss Norris! No, no, you'll be far safer with me to deal with your baggage, your meals and your overnight stops, I promise you.'

'Of course we shall. Don't be foolish, Van,' Mathilda recommended briskly. 'Have you breakfasted, Jerome? Do you really think the weather too foul for us to set forward today? Then perhaps we might play cards, or charades, or something to pass the time.'

'You might, I'm going for a walk,' Vanessa said firmly. She glanced at Jerome's boots. 'Is the snow very deep? I've boots, of course, but I don't relish getting snow over the tops!'

'The stable boy has dug a path across the yard, and the road is reasonable,' Jerome answered. 'What do you want to go out for? Is there something I might be able to obtain for you?'

'Yes, a book for Mercy, if you could find one,' Vanessa said promptly. 'Is there anything to read in your luggage?'

'No, but I could . . .' he hesitated, shooting an odd glance at Vanessa. 'I'll tell you what, if you're desirous of getting some fresh air, why not walk to the local manor, or the parsonage?

Doubtless the squire's lady or the parson's wife would be glad to lend you some volumes.'

'Yes, I'll do that,' Vanessa decided. She glanced enquiringly at Mathilda. 'Do you not wish to accompany me, Matty? It looks a pleasant day, a walk would not harm us.'

'No, I'll wait until the snow clears,' Mathilda said. 'Anyway, it would not do for both of us to go and leave Mercy unattended.'

Vanessa agreed, then glanced at Jerome, who was mending a pen. He looked up, waved the pen and said: 'You'll be off, then! I must write to Sir Thomas to inform him why we're delayed. Later in the day I'll send the letter to the coaching inn where it can remain until the first London-bound vehicle leaves.'

Vanessa, nothing loth, hurried up to the room she shared with Mercy, put on the boots she had borrowed from her cousin Charlie and her large cloak, tied a handkerchief cornerwise around her head, and set off.

It was so delightful out of doors that for the first ten minutes all she could do was to drink in the heady, iced wine of the air and rejoice in the sunshine. How glorious it was to be striding across the soft snow beside the road, then onto the narrow strip of cleared carriageway! She moved briskly, humming a song to herself, then bent and made a snowball which she threw at the snowy hedge, bringing down a miniature snow-storm and sending a robin bursting into the sky with a twitter of alarm.

An ancient man, sitting outside a cottage and basking in the sun, called 'Marnin', Missie!' so she went over to ask him the whereabouts of the parsonage.

'For my friend's abigail is ill, and wishes to borrow some books,' she concluded.

'Parson's not wed, Missie,' the old man said at length, having given the matter some thought. 'You'd best try Squire Fortescue's place, for old Leddy Fortescue's a great reader, I'm told. When she hears the gal's sick, she'll likely tek in a basket of comforts. Oh, a proper kind leddy she is!'

'Very well. But can you tell me the way to the manor?'

'Now let me see . . . You won't want to get your li'l feetsies wet, eh?'

'I'm wearing stout boots,' Vanessa said, lifting the hem of her already dripping skirt and displaying them.

'Oh ah, so you be! Well, tek the left-'and turn ahead, follow the road till you comes to a pair of gateposts wi' draggins on 'em, and 'tis straight ahead. That's the front way, o' course.'

'I see. Is that the quickest way?'

'Bless you no, Missie. Quickest is to turn past this 'ere cottage, down the lane till you comes to a stile. Hop you over it, crawst the medder, through the kissin' gate and you're in the garding. But you'll git turrble wet!'

'Thank you,' Vanessa said. 'I'll go that way.'

Having had experience of the garbled directions sometimes given by village ancients, she treated his directions with a certain amount of caution, but soon realised that the old man had been accurate both in his directions and in his prediction that she would get 'turrble wet'. Indeed, by the time she had crossed the lawn she was soaked to the knees, her green skirt dark with melted snow and her feet very cold indeed, despite the boasted boots.

She looked a little doubtfully down at herself. What a fright she must look, for the wind which blew so gently and delightfully had nevertheless brought her hair out of its neat knot, and tendrils of shining copper fell across her brow. She wondered whether to go round to the front door, or whether to try to find the kitchen premises, and was still wondering when a voice addressed her.

'I say, beauty in distress! Can I help you, ma'am? Do step inside!'

She glanced round and saw a young man in his mid-twenties with a cheerful, tanned face and thick, fair hair, regarding her from a nearby doorway. It was a garden door, made of glass and not much used in the winter, so she hurried towards him, her face burning, feeling very foolish.

'I do beg your pardon, suddenly arriving in your garden in such a manner! But you should not have opened the doors and let the cold into your . . . your library!'

Over his shoulder, now that she was near enough, she could see shelves laden with books, a thickly carpeted floor, and a brisk wood fire.

'Not at all. Do come inside.'

He led her into the warm and pleasant room, then shut the door and turned towards her, hand held out.

'We must introduce ourselves I fear, since your delightfully unconventional approach to my home has done away with formality! I am John Fortescue. And you, ma'am . . .'

'I'm Miss Vanessa —' she hesitated, suddenly remembering her *incognito*. 'Miss Vanessa Norris.'

They shook hands, and Vanessa glanced approvingly around her.

'How delightful this is, for I came to beg your Mama's indulgence over the matter of a book. Is Lady Fortescue at home? You see, my friend and I are staying at the Falcon Inn in the village, and my friend's abigail broke her leg when our coach overturned. She — the abigail I mean — is most dreadfully bored, and asked me to try to furnish her with some reading matter. I intended to visit the parsonage but an elderly gentleman in the village assured me that your parson is unmarried but that your Mama is a great reader. So I rather hoped Lady Fortescue might . . . might . . .'

'You hoped she might lend you some books, of course,' he concluded for her. 'My mother would be only too delighted, but I fear I shall have to be her proxy, for at present she's staying with my sister, who's in a delicate condition. However, all her books are on the shelves to the right of the fireplace, and I'm sure we can find something to amuse your woman.'

He turned to the shelves in question, tugging on the bell pull as he did so.

'You'll take some refreshment of course, after your walk? Some wine, perhaps, and a few biscuits? Or we might be able to find some macaroons. This is a bachelor household whilst my mother is away, but we aren't completely uncivilised, you'll find!'

A butler with a fatherly face appeared, looking a little startled to find his master entertaining a female guest who must have seemed, to him, to have appeared out of nowhere, but Squire Fortescue was an easy man with dependants and unexpected visitors alike.

'Ah, Hughes, this is Miss Norris, who has visited us to borrow some books. Would you bring us some wine and biscuits — you'll know what to provide for a young lady who has walked all the way from the Falcon, through the snow in Coggett's Lane!'

'Yes, indeed, sir.' The butler returned Vanessa's smile. 'I daresay a piece of plum cake would not come amiss.'

'And now Miss Norris, let us examine the books.'

The squire and Vanessa began to search the crowded shelves, Vanessa uttering an exclamation of pleasure at the sight of one particular volume.

'Oh, your mama has *The Castle of Otranto*! It is all the rage, I know, for my cousin was much impressed with her copy, and Mercy did mention that she very much desired to read it. And what about *Pamela*? That sounds just the sort of thing to amuse someone laid up with a broken leg.'

'Yes, indeed, and here is a work by Smollett which might help to beguile the hours. And another, by Jonathan Swift.' The squire glanced with some concern at the heavy volumes he had been piling into Vanessa's eager arms. 'I say, Miss Norris, I really cannot allow you to struggle back to the Falcon with such a load, nor can I offer to accompany you, for I'm expecting a friend for luncheon. However, I can send you home in my coach, and will do so with the greatest of pleasure.'

'I'm determined to walk, thank you,' Vanessa said firmly. 'I have no desire to arrive back at the inn too soon for I've been so bored, shut up with the snow keeping me imprisoned. But if you wouldn't mind, I could call again tomorrow for the rest of the books, and today merely carry away *Otranto*.'

'A capital plan! Except that I will wait on you at the inn later this afternoon. How does that seem? It will be a pleasant change for me, and perhaps you and your companion might honour me by dining with me? I assure you, to entertain two young ladies would give me a great deal of pleasure.'

'Well, I don't quite know . . .' Vanessa began, but was interrupted.

'You think a threesome would be poor sport, I daresay! Never fear, my friend Mr Collis is the curate's elder son, and I'm sure he would be delighted to accept an invitation to dine, and to meet you and your companion.'

'Oh no, that is, my friend, Miss Randolph, is accompanied, in a sense, by a young relative . . . well, a sort of . . . I believe he is a cousin . . .' stammered Vanessa. 'In short, sir, a Mr Jerome Harcourt is to escort us to London, and . . .'

'Capital!' beamed the squire. 'I'll invite Mr Harcourt too, of course. Then it's arranged. I will wait on your friend and yourself later in the day, bringing with me the other volumes for your maid.'

Whilst she was gratefully accepting this suggestion the butler re-entered the room and Vanessa, who had not realised how hungry and thirsty she was until she smelt the rich fruit cake and tasted the wine, made a hearty repast and then bade her host goodbye, thanking him for his kindness and assuring him that she and Miss Randolph would took forward to his visit with great pleasure.

Once outside again, however, and crossing the first snowy pasture, she blew out her cheeks. What a very persistent young man he was, and how hearty! But he was kind, and she suspected that if the bad weather continued, not only Mercy would be grateful for any diversion, even that of literature!

CHAPTER FIVE

With the book under one arm and a hand holding her skirt up above the snow, Vanessa trudged manfully back the way she had come. Her thoughts were beginning to be preoccupied by the fire she would certainly find in the coffee room, and the hot drink which she would immediately order to sustain her, when she heard the whimpering.

It came from a thicket of gorse quite close at hand and she glanced uneasily towards the sound, wondering whether it could be some poor creature caught in a trap. If it was, would she have the courage — or indeed, the knowledge — to despatch it? She rather feared not.

Hesitating, the whimper came again. A sort of low, sobbing sound, as if someone were too worn out and disspirited to stop themselves crying out at the cruelty of the world.

Resolutely, Vanessa stepped over to the thicket and, bending low, peered into the centre of the gorse where, as she knew from youthful experience, she would find a clear patch.

Lying on its side, with one paw caught in an ugly looking trap, was a very small, very skinny mongrel dog.

'I'm coming lad, I'm coming!' Vanessa called instantly. She had always loved dogs, and did not hesitate for a moment. Dropping to her knees, she crawled and wriggled her way into the thicket, arriving, panting and dishevelled, beside the small animal, who looked at her out of pain-filled eyes and uttered what it no doubt considered to be a ferocious growl, but which actually came out like a half-hearted mutter.

'That's right, you tell me off! Some very cruel person is responsible for this, and it might easily be me! You aren't to know I've come to rescue you,' Vanessa said cheerfully. She put her borrowed book down, seized the trap in both hands, and hauled it apart just enough for the dog's paw to slip out. Then she released the jaws of the trap and threw it clumsily into the gorse.

'What a terrible thing! Now, my boy, let's have a look at you!'

Closer inspection showed that the mongrel was an attractive little creature with curly white fur and a pair of bright brown eyes, but starvation and living rough had not improved his looks. His ribs stuck out, there were sores on his belly and on the mangled leg which had been in the trap, and his fur was rough and staring.

'But you'll be handsome once you've put on

84

some flesh, and had your wounds treated,' Vanessa promised him. She tucked him into the crook of her arm and proceeded to crawl out of the gorse once more, devoutly hoping that no one would see her, for she guessed that she must present a very unladylike picture.

Once standing up in the open, she arranged dog and book to her satisfaction and then took stock of her situation. She was now dirty and be-draggled in addition to being well soaked, and burdened as she was, she could not even tidy herself properly, for she dared not put her little dog down. Under the gorse the snow had been unable to penetrate but here it was so thick that the poor little creature would simply sink out of sight, and all his trust in her would be lost.

'Never mind, there's a side door to the inn which I'll wager is rarely used,' Vanessa in-formed her companion. 'We'll go very quietly round that way and hope to get to our room un-observed.' She remembered that her room was shared by Mathilda's abigail and added hope-fully, 'I'll introduce you to Mercy, and I daresay she's fond of dogs as well as of books!'

The dog reached up, his black, rubbery nose quivering, and licked her chin.

Vanessa laughed. 'Foolish creature, it's a bath I need, not a wash! Now here's the inn, little fellow, where you are to live for a day or so. We'll just go a little carefully here.'

She suited action to her words, melting as un-obtrusively as possible into a number of laurel bushes, snow-laden, which grew close to the side windows.

A movement in one window drew her attention and she froze, standing quite still amongst the bushes. Then she stared. It was Mathilda, an apron round her middle, stirring something in a small pudding basin. Even as Vanessa watched, another figure moved into view, coming round the door and closing it gently behind him. Jerome. He stood for a moment, leaned against the door, then said something which caused Mathilda to swing round, waving her spoon at him, half laughing, half menacing.

It was like a play, Vanessa thought, a mime in which no words could be heard and actions spoke for themselves. And no sooner had the thought formed, than Jerome stepped forward, plucked the spoon from Mathilda's grasp and took her by the shoulders, gradually drawing her closer to him whilst he looked down into the large blue eyes raised to his.

Vanessa knew what must come. She longed to run away, but she was frozen, an unwilling audience. Slowly, so slowly, Jerome's head lowered itself nearer to Mathilda's. His dark eyes held her gaze, Vanessa could see his fingers tightening their grasp on her friend's shoulders, so that by the time their lips met their bodies were fused, it seemed, into one.

Beneath her arm, the little dog wriggled and gave a subdued yelp. It brought Vanessa to her senses and, not waiting to see how long the kiss would continue, she dodged back into the bushes and moved nearer to her destination, which was the side door.

She comforted the dog as she did so, telling him how sorry she was to have squeezed him, rubbing his rough head against her chin, trying to ignore the confusion of pain and shock which the scene she had just witnessed had aroused in her.

She slipped through the side door and made straight for the back stairs. As she mounted them, anger was growing. False! He was false! She might not know a great deal about men, but she did know that men of honour did not kiss one girl one moment and another the next! He had played with her and now he meant to play with Mathilda!

A small gasp from her companion informed her that she was squeezing him again and she stopped in the dark corridor to kiss the top of his head and try to calm herself. For some reason her knees felt quite weak, and beneath the anger, which buoyed her up, misery was lurking.

'What shall we call you?' she asked the dog. 'Prince is a nice name, but you don't look much like a prince! Or we might try Nip, or . . .'

She was at the door of her bedchamber and opened it cautiously.

'Mercy? Are you awake? I've brought you a visitor!'

Mercy, propped up on pillows and rather list-lessly mending a piece of lace, glanced round and gave a slight scream.

'Miss, whatever have you got there? Gracious me, what a dirty . . . ooh, the poor thing, look at 'is leg! Here, old fellow, let Mercy see.'

'It's a dog,' Vanessa said rather unnecessarily. 'It was caught in a trap. I'm pretty sure the leg isn't broken, but the poor creature needs treatment. And feeding and affection, of course.'

'Poor fellow! You'd better take 'im down to the stables, because they'll have salves and suchlike. Mind you, what . . .' Mercy broke off, staring at Vanessa. 'Oh, Miss, what 'ave you been a-doing?'

Vanessa grimaced at her reflection in the glass. 'Rescuing this fellow from a gorse patch! Look, I dare not go downstairs in this state, might I put the dog on the rug by the fire for a bit, whilst I change and tidy myself?'

'You can put 'im on the bed,' Mercy said.

'You are good! But I don't think I should do that; he's probably absolutely crawling with lice and fleas and pests of that nature. I'll get him bathed as soon as I'm able.'

'I never thought of that,' Mercy admitted. 'Lie 'im on the rug then. What'll you do, Miss? Ring for some 'ot water? Mind you, Miss Mathilda will be up soon; she's got hold of a recipe for a soothing posset which she wanted to try on me.' She chuckled and glanced at the dog. 'If he's 'ungry, he might as well eat it as me; we've both been in the wars!'

'I'll wash in cold, I think,' Vanessa decided. 'Landladies can be very odd about animals kept in the rooms, and one has to admit he's dirty! What shall we call him, Mercy?'

She poured cold water into the basin as she spoke, stripped off her dripping cloak and then shed her gown and standing in her clean though very wet petticoat, began vigorously to wash.

Mercy declared herself quite unable to think of any name for their new aquisition other than Whitey, which Vanessa rejected with scorn, and watched as the other gradually became clean and neat once more, with her hair brushed out and tied back, her skin gleaming and her boots cast aside for velvet slippers. She noticed Vanessa was very pale, that her eyes had a strained look, but put it down to the miserable business with the trap.

'Do you 'ave another gown, Miss?' she enquired, as Vanessa ruefully held up the draggled green garment and began to brush at the skirt. 'If not, why not borrow one of Miss Matty's? She wouldn't grudge it, as I'm sure you know.'

Vanessa was beginning to answer when the door burst open without ceremony and Mathilda bustled in, a bowl held carefully between her hands.

'Here it is, Mercy! Now eat it up and you'll feel much more the thing,' she cried. 'I've made it. . . . Gracious, Van, whatever are you doing in your petticoat?'

'I've got a bit wet,' Vanessa said, striving to make her voice sound normal. 'We were wondering . . .'

'A bit wet? That gown is not only soaked, it's filthy! You must borrow one of mine, goodness knows I've got plenty with me. Which do you think would suit Miss Vanessa, Mercy? You know which gowns would be easiest to reach. And a clean petticoat, otherwise you'll catch your death!'

'It's very kind of you,' Vanessa said. For the life of her, she could not make her voice sound natural! 'Any gown will do, truly, until my own things are dry.'

She glanced at Mathilda, seeing the flushed cheeks and bright eyes, knowing the cause, hating herself for the way she felt.

'That's arranged then! Which gown, Mercy?'

'There's a leaf-brown one on top, Miss,' Mercy said. 'That would be nice, over a dark yellow petticoat. And I think there is a dark yellow velvet ribbon which would look well in Miss's hair.'

'Thank you . . .' Vanessa began, but was interrupted.

'What a poppet! Where did he spring from? You *dear* little dog, what's your name, then?'

Mathilda bent over the dog, very pretty and gracious in her sprigged gold and white gown, and cooed affectionately. The dog, startled by the rush of perfume and sudden proximity of another young woman, curled his lip and growled tentatively.

Glad to be able to change the subject from that of her dress, Vanessa explained the dog's presence, adding that she was about to take it down

90

to the stables for a bath and some medicaments for its many wounds.

'He's nervous of me, you'd better carry him, but I'll come with you,' Mathilda declared at once. 'We'll call Jerome, shall we? He won't mind spreading the stuff on his sores.'

'I'll see to him, thanks. He's my responsibility,' Vanessa said sharply. 'I won't trouble Mr Harcourt.'

Mathilda raised her delicately pencilled brows. 'Mr Harcourt now, is it? My, what's he done to descend to that? You were friendly enough yesterday.'

'Oh dear, did I sound sharp? I'm sorry, I didn't mean to be. But nevertheless, the dog is my responsibility, you must agree I cannot ask Jerome to take care of him.' This reminded Vanessa of something else. She clapped a hand to her head. 'I'll forget my own name in a minute! Mercy, I visited the manor and procured a book for you. It's on the chair.' She picked up the volume and proffered it to Mercy, who took it eagerly. 'Yes, it is *Otranto*, as you requested, and the squire, Mr Fortescue, is coming to visit us later in the afternoon and bringing some more volumes. They were too much for me to carry.'

Mercy's cry of delight and her thanks took several moments, in the course of which Mathilda slipped out of the room, and returned with the gown and petticoat.

It was the work of a moment for Vanessa to put them on, tie the yellow ribbon in her hair, and

91

then pick up the small dog.

'I'll bring him up again when he's respectable,' she assured the abigail. 'In the meantime, enjoy your book!'

The two girls went down to the stables, where the stable boy, having been enjoying a snooze in the hay, was glad enough to offer to bath and bind up the dog's hurts in exchange for the largesse offered.

'I'll stay with you,' Vanessa said firmly however, having no faith in the stable boy's ability to bathe the small animal with sufficient care. The girls watched as water was poured into a tin bath, strong lye soap produced, and the dog stood on three legs in the tub, whining and shivering, but obedient to Vanessa's demand that he 'Stay, like a good fellow!'

It was when the three of them were endeavouring to dry the animal with handfuls of loose dry hay that Jerome walked into the stable.

'What a domestic scene!' he remarked drily, suddenly appearing in the empty stall they had chosen for the task. 'Where did you get that cur?'

'He isn't . . .' began Vanessa, but was interrupted by a triumphant crow from Mathilda.

'Curly! That's a nice name for you, Van! And then, when rude gentlemen call him a cur, you can pretend it's short for Curly!'

'Curly is rather nice,' Vanessa admitted grudgingly. 'See how his fur really does curl? He looks very sweet now, all white and fluffy!'

Jerome moved forward and bent to examine

Curly's leg. 'Been in a trap, old fellow?' He turned to the stable boy. 'What do you intend to put on those sores?'

A technical discussion then ensued between the two men, at the end of which Jerome, armed with a tin of disgusting looking grease, bent and annointed Curly's legs and belly and then suggested, in a somewhat bored tone, that they had best repair to the inn where they would find a nuncheon laid out, the hot soup which formed part of the repast being doubtless both cold and congealed by now.

'Curly needs food first,' Vanessa said quickly. 'You two go ahead and I'll take him into the kitchen.'

Jerome had not failed to notice that she would not meet his eyes and hesitated, then took Mathilda's arm and led her back to the coffee room. Whatever had annoyed Vanessa would be of short duration, he was sure. After all, the girl had no idea that he intended to pursue her friend with every wile at his command! This was the best opportunity of marrying an heiress which had ever come his way or was ever likely to do so! If he ruined it, he would only have himself to blame. But he did not intend to ruin it. Every time he grew bored with Mathilda's conversation, every time he thought her looks insipid beside some women he knew, he conjured up in his mind a picture of his home. The neglected farms, the over-run garden, the tenants, eking out a miserable existence in leaky and tumbledown cottages, because he could not afford to put things right. He owed it to everyone to marry well!

Jerome had a good opinion of his own ability to attract women, but he knew that closetted with him in a rural inn, and then in a coach, an intimacy and a dependance on his company could grow up which would be impossible in London, at his uncle's house.

The best of it was, he thought now, that whilst the two girls vied for his attentions, even if they did so unknowingly, there was no other male for miles to enter the lists! He knew Vanessa liked him — how much deeper her feelings might be he was not prepared to consider — and he knew, also, that Mathilda was dazzled by his attention and his air of being a man of the world; by his reputation as a rake and a libertine, even.

The kiss in the scullery had been a natural re-action of one left alone with a pretty girl, but he had considered very carefully before even entering the scullery that morning. Knowing that Vanessa was out had decided him to act whilst the coast was clear. He had already decided that, if necessary, he would persuade Mathilda to run away with him, thus compromising her so thoroughly that she would be compelled to marry him and her Papa compelled to accept the match with complacency. But to do so before Vanessa's wide, shocked green eyes was more than even he could stomach!

Damn Vanessa, he thought crossly now, his

hand cupping Mathilda's elbow as he led her into the coffee room. Why must she enter my life and disturb me so? She is pretty and lively, spirited and cuddly — and the last person I must think of marrying!

Rather to Vanessa's disappointment, the landlady failed to recognise, at a glance, Curly's many charms.

'Get that dawg out of 'ere!' she commanded, upon walking into her kitchen and seeing Curly, head down, making short work of a plate of scraps. 'Oh, beg pardon, Miss, I'm sure, I didn't see you a-standin' there.'

'I'm afraid I brought the dog in, Mrs Lubbock,' Vanessa said with her most winning smile. 'He's been caught in a trap and was starving hungry, so I cleaned him up and now I've brought him in here for something to eat.'

'Oh. Well, it'll 'ave to sleep in the stables,' Mrs Lubbock said. 'I don't want to be unchristian, Miss, but we've 'ouse rules and no dawgs is one of 'em.' Unbending a little as Vanessa turned large, dismayed eyes upon her, she added: 'Not but what he looks a good little feller! He can sleep in th'end stall.'

Bowing to the inevitable, Vanessa allowed Curly to finish his meal and to have a long drink of water, then she picked him up once more and carried him out to the stables.

'Mrs Lubbock won't let me keep him indoors,' she explained to the stable boy. 'But if you would be kind enough to keep an eye on him and stop him from running away, I'll give you a guinea when we leave.'

The stable boy assured Vanessa that it would be a pleasure to keep an eye on the little dog, though honesty compelled him to assure her that no dog as intelligent as Curly would run away from a warm bed at night and three good meals a day.

'Perhaps not,' Vanessa conceded, 'I shall visit him often, of course. And if this thaw continues, we may well leave tomorrow or the day after.'

When she returned to the coffee room, it was to find Mathilda in a rather vexed frame of mind and Jerome nowhere to be seen.

'Wherever have you been? Mathilda demanded as soon as Vanessa entered the room. 'We waited and waited, and then since you didn't appear and Jerome and I were just about starving, we ate without you.'

'That's all right, I wasn't hungry,' Vanessa said truthfully. 'I just looked in to tell you I'd left Curly in the stable, and now I'm going up to see how Mercy does.'

'Well, you cannot; the doctor's with her.'

Vanessa came further into the room and looked curiously at her friend.

'What's the matter, Matty? Do you feel out of sorts? When we were bathing Curly you seemed so happy but now it seems you're blue-devilled!'

'It's Jerome,' Mathilda admitted. 'Do you know, Van, he can be *most* unreasonable? He suggested that, since the thaw seemed to be continuing, we might go for a ride this afternoon, I upon your Bullfinch and he upon his stallion. Then I remembered you said Mr Fortescue was to call upon us, and intended to invite us to dine. Naturally, I told him that we could not abandon you, and he looked very put out, stared at me for a minute, and then said "Hell and the devil confound it!" and turned and walked out of the room!'

'That was unreasonable,' Vanessa agreed. 'However, it was a compliment, Matty! He would obviously much rather ride with you than talk with Squire Fortescue.'

'There is that, I suppose,' Mathilda said, her eyes beginning to sparkle. 'But to leave me so rudely! It isn't a gentlemanly way to behave, Van!'

Vanessa smiled to herself. She was beginning to see that, if Jerome was really intent for some reason upon persuading Mathilda to fall in love with him, the intervention of Squire Fortescue could not be welcome. Then it occurred to her that Jerome had no idea that the squire was young, good looking and unmarried. So why had he been so incensed to hear of the proposed visit?

She was still wondering when, after a preliminary tap, the doctor entered the room.

'Your maid is in good heart, and needs no more of my potions,' he greeted Mathilda cheerfully. 'Indeed, except that she must try not to move her leg unduly, I would say she might leave here tomorrow! But as it is, she should remain in bed for several weeks.'

'When can I carry her back to London, then?' Mathilda said, pouting. 'I suppose I could engage another abigail temporarily . . .'

'I'm afraid you'll have to do so, ma'am,' the doctor said apologetically. 'It would be most unwise to move her, and in any case she will not be able to do her work for many weeks.'

'Well, I suppose I'd better make arrangements with the landlady to take care of Mercy, and when she is well enough, doctor, perhaps you could despatch her to London, on the stage?'

'Yes, I'm sure that would be in order, ma'am. No one would expect you to incur all the trouble and expense of remaining here now that she is well.'

The doctor bowed himself out and Vanessa said curiously, 'I wonder what ordinary people do when they break their legs on a journey? I mean you can perfectly well afford to pay for Mercy's bed and board and for any extras she may need, but how do ordinary people go on?'

'I neither know nor care,' Mathilda said airily. 'Van, a most handsome young man just came in through the main door whilst the doctor was leaving. I wonder who it is?'

'Is he tall, with fair hair?'

'Why, yes! Curly fair hair. Don't say . . .'

'Yes, that will be the squire,' Vanessa agreed, her eyes twinkling. 'I forgot to tell you he was neither old nor wed! Shall we go into the hall to meet him?'

'No, we had better wait here. Surely Mrs Lubbock will direct him in here?'

To their surprise, however, it was Jerome who presently ushered the squire into the room, a Jerome very urbane and elegant in dark brown velvet, the fall of lace at his throat emphasising his dark and dangerous countenance. Beside him, Squire Fortescue looked excessively English, very good-natured and a trifle bucolic.

Jerome called for wine and when the invitation to dine was extended, said that for his part he would be delighted to accept but that it was up to his fair companions to make up his mind for him.

'For since the snow is thawing so rapidly, there's a chance that we might leave tomorrow morning, and that would mean an early start,' he explained.

Any hopes he might have cherished of Vanessa and Mathilda heeding this warning were doomed to disappointment, however.

'We can still dine with Mr Fortescue and be back in good time,' Vanessa said gaily. 'What do you think, Mathilda?'

She ignored the look of deep loathing which Jerome shot at her and was rewarded by Mathilda's enthusiastic agreement.

'It would be very pleasant, and we accept,' Mathilda said.

'Excellent. My coach will call for you in plenty

of time, and, naturally, you will be carried back to the inn at whatever hour you feel appropriate,' the squire said gallantly.

A time was agreed upon, the wine drunk, and the squire departed, leaving behind him the promised books for the sufferer.

'Well, that's going to be a pleasant way to spend the evening,' Vanessa observed rather maliciously, after the squire had left. 'Now I'm going to check on Curly's bandage.'

She smiled graciously at Jerome, who gave her a hard and enigmatic stare, and went out to the stables, considerably puzzled. What *was* Jerome's game? Why on earth should he object to their spending an innocent evening at the manor, being entertained by a young bachelor of impeccable lineage and excellent manners? He had not let his feelings show to either the squire or Mathilda, but she knew him well enough by now to interpret his expressions.

She was soon to find out.

She had been in the stable barely five minutes when Jerome strode in, went over and checked that Terror was all right, and then came into the stall where she stood, watching Curly demolishing another plate of scraps as though he had not eaten for a week.

'I suppose you're feeling very pleased with yourself?'

Vanessa glanced up at his brooding face, her own reflecting her innocence.

'Not especially. Why?'

'You can't wait to get Mathilda away from me, can you? You know she's already half in love with me, and you don't want her to go the rest of the way. Though what I've done to you to deserve such shabby treatment . . .'

'I don't know what you're talking about!' Vanessa declared, stung. 'As for getting Mathilda away from you, I've never even thought about it! She's got a father to take care of her, and this Godmama she's going to stay with, and a heap of other well-wishers. Why should I interfere?'

He was still staring at her, but with less aggression than before.

'Yes, why? Could it be misguided friendship? If so, I promise you, Vanessa, that Mathilda will be as happy married to me as . . .'

'Married to you? Did you say *married?* Jerome, you must have taken leave of your senses! I've no doubt Mathilda intends to marry, and probably she would quite like to marry you, but she's been looking forward to entering society ever since we first met, more than two years ago. She isn't going to get married until she's had plenty of enjoyment!'

Jerome continued to stare at her.

'Yes, but . . . I'd take her to London, give her a good time! I don't see why that wouldn't suffice.'

Vanessa moved nearer to him, her expression earnest. 'Jerome, you are so experienced, yet you know *nothing* about young women! It isn't the dances and the parties which are so enjoyable, it is being courted and pursued by half-a-dozen eligible and ineligible young men! As your wife, poor Mathilda would be out of the running! Oh, if she was head over ears in love with you that wouldn't matter. But she isn't, and won't be! She isn't a very impulsive girl, you see. And please don't blame me for what isn't my fault!'

It was quiet in the stables. The stable boy and groom were in the kitchen having a meal and apart from the occasional restive moment from one of the horses, they might have been miles from anywhere. Vanessa, watching Jerome's face, saw it change. The look in his eyes had been hard, abstracted, but now his glance softened even as his hands shot out and caught her shoulders. She said nothing, continuing to watch him steadily, but he saw her lips tighten and smiled mockingly.

'You think me contemptible, to want to marry Mathilda on such short acquaintance,' he said in a low voice. 'But, by God, necessity teaches one how to treat the gentler emotions! If it wasn't for necessity it would be *you* who was in danger here, not Mathilda.'

She opened her mouth to answer sharply, but he released her so suddenly that she nearly fell over, and whilst she regained her balance he turned on his heel and left her.

She walked back to Curly, who had finished his meal and was lying down in the hay again, slowly and thoughtfully biting the bandage off his front leg. Already it was hanging in a soggy, tangled strip and Vanessa bent over him, untied it completely and reached for a fresh strip of the linen which had been used.

'Bad boy, don't take it off,' she murmured, carefully winding the linen round the skinny little leg. She continued to talk to Curly as she worked, but her mind was in a turmoil.

What on earth did Jerome mean, that necessity taught one to . . . she could no longer remember his exact words, because there had been no sense in them. And why should he seem to imply that Mathilda was in danger, just because she, Vanessa, had said that the other girl would not marry him? It did not make sense.

She finished the bandaging and stood up to leave the stable, then stood stock-still as a thought struck her.

Suppose it did make sense? Suppose Jerome *was* a fortune hunter, despite her confident denial to Mathilda? And suppose he had decided to abduct Mathilda? She felt herself turn deathly cold. If he did so, the fault would be hers! It would be she who had assured him so confidently that Mathilda would never marry him until she had enjoyed her Season, she who had killed that hope!

And what of the other remark? If it wasn't for necessity it would be *you* who was in danger here, not Mathilda, he had said. She could not help her heart giving a tiny leap as she thought the words over. Then he did like her! Better than he liked Mathilda at any rate. She shook herself

103

briskly. It was both stupid and pointless to think thoughts like that! She must get back to the inn and make very sure that, whatever his intentions, he did not ruin Mathilda for his own selfish ends!

She picked up Curly's empty dish, bade the little dog to be a good boy and not to eat his lovely bandage, and went thoughtfully towards the inn.

CHAPTER
SIX

Vanessa was sure that she was right; Jerome neither loved nor desired Mathilda, but for the sake of her fortune he would abduct her and force her into marriage. She was shocked, even horrified, but she was also a practical girl. A very little thought soon convinced her that a great many marriages amongst the upper classes were undertaken for the self-same reasons that had caused Jerome to consider abduction. The man needed money, the woman wanted a respectable husband with an honoured name. No one thought any the worse of dukes who married the daughters of merchant princes, or the sons of merchant princes who married earl's daughters! Even the so-called 'love matches', where young men and women of the Beau Monde met at the parties and dances during the Season, were usually undertaken with both eyes wide open — and fixed on the main chance! How many pretty but penniless younger daughters married well? Very few, Vanessa knew from her aunt's conversation.

So though she could not help being shocked by what Jerome was contemplating, she did feel some sympathy for him. He had been driven to it, perhaps, by circumstances which she could not understand. She was prepared to believe him thoughtless, selfish even, but not deliberately wicked. Therefore, she decided, she could not warn Mathilda of her suspicions.

For she had known her friend quite long enough to realise that the older girl would be incapable of keeping such a confidence to herself. She might not believe, at first, but once she accepted that Jerome was willing to abduct her so that she would be forced to marry him, nothing would exceed her fury, nor the speed with which she would spread the story around.

And Vanessa found that ruining Jerome was something which she was not prepared to do, even for Mathilda's sake. After all, he had not ruined her when he might easily have done so, and she knew that, in her innocence, she must have made it clear that she wanted him.

So what to do? As she dressed for dinner with the squire, darkening her brows and lightly powdering her copper curls, her worries brought a crease to Vanessa's brow, until Mathilda asked if she had the headache and would rather be excused the party.

'No, no, I'm quite all right, only a little tired,' Vanessa assured her. But it was not true. She could not think what to do for the best but knew she could not let Mathilda step into whatever trap Jerome intended to lay for her. The question was, what trap? How did he intend to lure Mathilda into a situation where he might compromise her? That the girl had welcomed his lovemaking he could not doubt after her surrender to his kisses in the scullery. Did he assume from that that Mathilda would willingly go further? If so, he was much mistaken, for Vanessa knew her friend well enough to know how outraged she would be by such a suggestion. Mathilda was a charming young lady, but she was neither impetuous nor romantic. Her heart, Vanessa was sure, would never rule her head.

Throughout the excellent dinner Vanessa was quieter than usual, though she ate with her usual good appetite. Her brain was busy, trying to see what to do for the best.

And then it was the squire who gave her the answer she sought.

Dinner over, she had accompanied him to his library to see if she could find some more books for the abigail. It had been arranged that the squire would take reading matter to the inn from time to time, and would keep Miss Randolph posted as to her servant's progress.

Now, in the quiet book-room, Mr Fortescue and his fair companion searched the shelves, talking quietly as they selected volumes for the unfortunate Mercy.

'Do ye know, Miss Norris, when you and Miss

Randolph came in at my door this evening, I was puzzled to recognise which was which? She being a yaller-head and you being a chestnut filly, I'd not thought you alike. Yet with powdered heads, I could scarcely tell one from t'other!'

'Yes, I suppose . . .' Vanessa said slowly. 'I'm wearing one of Miss Randolph's gowns and it has required no alteration. Yes, I do see . . .'

'You could have been twin-sisters,' the squire continued. 'Both pretty, both fair! I declare I might have been looking in a mirror, from one to t'other!'

It was food for thought, Vanessa reflected, after they had rejoined the other couple. To take Mathilda's place! But when? When would Jerome decide that he had wasted enough time and must pounce now or lose his chance of marrying the heiress?

Presently the talk turned to their journey, and Jerome told the company that he had made enquiries and had tentatively booked them a coach for the morrow.

'We shall leave betimes,' he warned them, 'So you'd best bid Mercy goodbye tonight. I'll be riding alongside the coach on my stallion, so I've not hired outriders.'

'And my groom and outriders will bring my coach and horses on to London when the coach is mended,' Mathilda said. 'Well, Mr Fortescue, I look forward to meeting you again in London, and repaying your delightful hospitality. May I send you a card for the ball to celebrate my entering society?'

Vanessa saw with a new and sad knowledge that Jerome seemed every bit as pleased over this ingenuous invitation as was the squire. Because, Vanessa thought bitterly, Jerome thinks that by the time Mathilda reaches London she'll be well and truly compromised, and on the point of becoming his wife.

However, she said nothing of her suspicions and they returned to the inn as arranged, the squire accompanying them to the very door, handing her across the dripping yard in the moonlight with the remark that spring was obviously coming with the thaw.

They parted good friends, with many promises to meet again soon, the squire striding back to his lonely manor house, Jerome going off to the stable to visit his horse, and the two girls to hurry up to their beds, for Jerome had warned them that he would send the chambermaid round early, to rouse them for the journey.

It was easy to bid farewell to Mercy, who had shared her room, though the woman was inclined to be tearful at the thought of being left. But presently she slept and Vanessa was free to lie on her back, staring at the mottling moonlight as it came through the shutters, and thinking.

When would Jerome strike? Should she even now be listening for his step? But further thought convinced her that he would probably make his move when they were actually journeying towards London once again. Probably he would make his move the following night. They would be much nearer London, yet not so near that help could be speedily summoned, and they would not be surrounded by people who knew them, as they now were at the Falcon. He could, of course, wait until they were nearer London still, but it would be an unnecessary risk.

Satisfied that the attempt would be made the following night, Vanessa settled down and slept at last.

The next day followed much the course Vanessa had expected. She, Mathilda and Curly were roused early and bundled into the coach whilst the sky was still barely grey with morning. They stopped briefly for refreshment, then pressed on again. It was the longest journey Vanessa had ever undertaken and also the most uncomfortable. The reason, she soon realised was that they were travelling faster than was wise on such bad roads; obviously Jerome had a destination in mind and was determined to reach it before nightfall, come what may!

During the stops, Vanessa had leisure to study Jerome, and concluded that attentive and charming though he undoubtably was, he was also . . . distant, thought Vanessa. As though he did not want to be forced into intimacy with either of them. I believe, Vanessa told herself, that he hates what he feels he must do!

Several times during the day, she hovered on

the verge of telling Mathilda. Oh, not that Jerome intended to abduct her, but that he wanted to marry her. How would she react? If she was willing, what a lot of trouble and heartache would be avoided! Once or twice the mention of marriage was made, but Mathilda was impatient with such far off eventualities. She wanted to talk of admirers, gowns and petticoats, conquests galore. She took it for granted that she would be much admired, much sought-after, and for the life of her Vanessa could not tell whether Mathilda accepted that it was the size of her fortune rather than the brightness of her eyes which would be the main cause of such admiration — or whether, knowing, she cared!

When it was almost dusk they passed an inn called the Tabor House and Vanessa noticed, without much interest, that Jerome was just issuing from the stables, calling some remark over his shoulder as he did so. For a moment she thought they would be spending the night there, but no, he overtook the coach presently, riding past with an uplifted hand but without indicating in any way that they were near journey's end.

It was dark by the time they eventually did leave the coach, at an inn called The Grapes, and no one was in a very good temper. Curly shot from the vehicle and stood, leg lifted and eyes fixed vaguely on the middle distance, relieving himself against the mounting block so that Vanessa, tired and stiff though she was, had no choice but to remain with him. Fortunately, the weather had remained mild and even springlike, but even so the scent of coffee, new-baked bread and roasting meat which came to her from the kitchens was very tempting, and she jerked hopefully on the short length of rope round Curly's neck a couple of times.

Jerome, coming from the stable where he had left Terror, grinned at her predicament.

'Busy, isn't he? Shall I take him whilst you join Mathilda in the coffee room?'

'No, thank you. He can't be much longer.' Vanessa bent and tickled Curly behind the ears. 'Ready?'

Curly seemed to consider for a moment, then shook himself vigorously, licked her hand, and trotted into the inn.

Jerome, following them into the coffee room, ordered coffee and biscuits and then advised them to get some rest before dinner.

'You must be worn out from all that bouncing along,' he said caressingly. 'But I did want to break the back of the journey today so that we should only have a short stage tomorrow. I've ordered dinner in two hours' time, so you can really rest. Does that mean I'm forgiven for rushing you along at such a pace?'

'Of course it does,' Mathilda said, giving him a coy glance. 'I'll give you the very first dance at my come-out ball.' Another glance. '*And* the second!'

Jerome laughed. 'That would set all the old

tabbies a-talking! You wouldn't want that, would you?'

He meant it jokingly, Vanessa was sure, but Mathilda gave the matter serious thought before replying.

'Would that make the old tabbies talk? Then of course I should not do it. I want to have a wonderful Season which people will talk of for years — the Season that Miss Randolph was toast of the Beau Monde! And then I want to marry someone very rich and very important!'

With one blow, Vanessa thought as they repaired to their rooms, Mathilda had sealed her fate! Whatever hopes Jerome may have cherished, now he would know that there was only one way to win this particular heiress!

There were two rooms, opposite each other. Vanessa took the room overlooking the front of the inn, washed her hands and face to get off some of the journey-dust, and then collapsed on the bed. But not to sleep. For a few minutes she lay supine, frowning at the ceiling, then she got cautiously to her feet and rang the bell. When the maid appeared, she asked her for pen, ink and paper, and sealing wax.

When her request had been complied with she sat down on the stool before the dressing table and wrote a short note, which she folded and sealed. She then slipped the letter into her dressing table drawer and went back to her bed, pushing Curly to one side, for he had taken advantage of her temporary absence to curl up blissfully in the hollow warmed by her body.

When the chambermaid came in to wake her with a cup of hot chocolate and a steaming jug of water for washing, she hesitated for a moment before calling her name. Miss Norris looked so tired and such a pretty thing, with her white face framed in glowing curls, that the girl felt it was unkind to disturb her.

The three of them dined well and sat around the fire afterwards, relaxing and chatting.

Jerome was quieter than usual. Several times Vanessa saw him looking at her but whenever she met his glance he looked quickly away. She guessed that he had not before considered what her feelings must be when she found herself deserted next morning, and was suffering all the pangs of guilt and unhappiness which one might expect. He was planning, if she was right, to leave her most unpleasantly circumstanced, and she was glad if he was suffering from remorse and a bad conscience. After all, if she had allowed his abduction of Mathilda to go ahead, she would have woken next morning to find herself quite alone — no coach, no escort, no chaperon, just her little dog!

How typical of a man, she thought scornfully, to give no thought to the muddle he would leave behind him! Now *her* plan had allowed for such contingencies! Poor Mathilda would not be left alone at the inn with no explanation. She would know what had happened (or rather, what

Vanessa wished her to believe had happened) and what to do next the moment she opened Vanessa's note!

'Does the noise from the inn kitchen bother you?' Jerome asked Mathilda solicitously presently. 'I noticed there was a good deal of noise going on whilst I waited for you to come down to dine.'

'No, for I was so tired that I slept until the chambermaid roused me,' Mathilda said at once. Vanessa, quietly smiling, realised that Jerome now knew without a shadow of doubt who was in which room.

'And you, Vanessa? Is your room quiet enough?'

'Yes, thank you. How near are we to London now, may I ask?'

'About twenty miles distant, I think. We should reach Hanover Square in time for a nuncheon if we set out early.'

'That is nice. Well, if we mean to make an early start, then we'd best be off to bed! Come, Curly!'

'I'll come as well,' Mathilda said. 'Then you can unfasten my gown for me, Van, and brush out my hair and so on. I do miss Mercy, even though she wasn't much use with a broken leg!'

Together the two girls mounted the stairs, with Curly tucked securely beneath his mistress's arm.

Presently, when Mathilda had been eased out of her gown and into her nightdress, had had her hair brushed out and tied in curl-papers and had washed herself, she climbed into bed and bade Vanessa goodnight.

'Goodnight, Matty. Listen, would you do me a favour?'

'Of course! Do you want me to unfasten you?'

Vanessa giggled. 'Of course not, I'm not useless, like you! No, but could you have Curly sleep in your room tonight? Just for once, dearest? Because I'm in the front and this afternoon whenever a coach arrived or departed, he barked. I know there won't be much coming and going whilst it's dark, but when it begins to get light I'll be constantly disturbed. Would you mind?'

'No, of course not. He won't start barking when the kitchen comes to life though, will he? Not that I should complain, when I think how good you were over Mercy. Come on, Curly, jump up here!'

She patted her bed and laughed at Curly, who gazed unenthusiastically at her for a moment, then yawned hugely and sat down for a good scratch.

'No, don't call him up now, I'll have to take him outside for a quick walk round the yard,' Vanessa reminded her.

'A quick stand by the mounting block, you mean. Don't be long then, or I shall be asleep!'

Vanessa made her way downstairs, then glanced into the coffee room. No one was there. Passing by the tap, however, she saw Jerome about to drink a glass of something brown and dark looking. She coughed, and when he looked up, said 'I'm taking Curly for his before-bed airing, Jerome. Will you come?'

Jerome hesitated, then drank up and joined her.

'Why this sudden desire for my company? I've had the feeling that I was in disgrace with you, for some strange reason!'

'How absurd!' The big green eyes turned up to his in the moonlight looked positively angelic. 'If I'm cross with anyone at the moment I'm cross with Matty. And I suppose if you hadn't put the idea into her head . . . But there, I musn't cry over split milk. Do you think we've been out long enough?'

'I imagine so. But what do you mean, you're annoyed with Mathilda? And why should it be my fault?'

He steered her in through the door, then detained her in the hall, his hand warm on her upper arm.

'Come along, what's the trouble, Vanessa?'

'No trouble, I'm only teasing. I've changed bedrooms with Matty because of what you said over the noise from the kitchens. She was afraid that when the maids got up in the morning they would disturb her,' Vanessa said mendaciously.

'Well I'm . . .' he looked genuinely horrified. 'She's a selfish creature, your friend.'

But Vanessa, denying it, knew that his horror had been for himself. She knew, now, that to-night was to be the night!

'Well, I hope you'll sleep sound anyway,

Vanessa. And try not to think too hardly of me.'

It might have meant anything, yet Vanessa never doubted the import of the message, nor the tender, rueful look in those dark eyes. But she could not let him know that the remark referred to anything but Mathilda's supposed self-ishness. She murmured something, bade him goodnight, and made her way up the stairs once more. At the top, she glanced back. He was standing at the foot of the stairs, gazing in front of him, but not as though he saw anything. His face looked stern.

The scratching at her door panel came no more than a couple of hours after she had settled down for the night — ostensibly, at any rate. Leaving Curly with Mathilda had not been as simple as she had hoped, for one thing. At first he had flatly refused to believe that she meant to leave him; every time she made for the door he had jumped off the bed and bustled after her, even barking sharply when she tried to close the door in his face.

But at last, after several attempts, he had seen reason and settled down on the foot of Mathilda's bed with a resigned expression on his shaggy face.

So now, the scratching on the door, and then a voice calling softly, 'Mathilda! Miss Randolph! Do wake up!'

She had not dared to sleep, partly for fear she should not wake when he came to her door, partly, it must be confessed, because she had powdered her hair so that she should look like Mathilda, and was afraid to wake with her own colour clearly showing and the pillow well floured! Now, she stirred, as if roused for the first time, then padded across the room, picked up her cloak and draped it round herself, and went to the door, opening it a crack.

'What is it? Is there a fire?'

She spoke quite loudly and the figure in the doorway put a finger to its lips. It was Jerome.

'Not so loud, you'll wake the whole house! No, it's nothing to be afraid of. It's that minx Vanessa!'

Obediently, she lowered her voice to a whisper. 'What on earth has she done? And why must I be told about it in the middle of the night?'

'She's run away again! That must have been why she asked me how near we were to London. Little fool, she's left me a note and has taken my horse. If you knew Terror you'd know that we might easily find her cast in the roadway with a broken neck! But she says she's gone to a friend in London. My dear, we must go after her!'

'Why? If it's what she wants . . .' Vanessa allowed her whisper to become a little peevish.

He grinned; she saw the flash of his teeth against the dark skin in the chancy moonlight.

'Dear innocence! You remember asking what would set all the tabbies talking? Why, it would set them talking to know that we were together at an inn, within twenty miles of London, without the whisper of a chaperon! That is why we must find Vanessa, and bring her back to give our journey respectability.'

'Of course!' She let it appear that she was much struck by this argument. 'I'll dress at once.'

'Good girl. As soon as I received the note I told the coachman to put the horses to and said we'd be ready to set out in ten minutes. Can you dress in that time?'

She began to agree, then said quickly, 'When did you receive the note? How long has she been gone?'

'She must have pushed it beneath my door, believing me to be asleep, but I was wakeful and heard the rustle. She has had a short start only, therefore.'

'Very well. I'll hurry.'

Ten minutes later they met in the moonlit stable yard. Vanessa was wearing Mathilda's thick, dark cloak, with the hood pulled well forward, though she knew that the white curls escaping from its edge would calm any doubts he might harbour. Not that he would harbour any — why should he?

He came forward and handed her tenderly into the coach, then climbed in beside her. He sat down opposite her, saying, 'I've told the man to go carefully, though it's safe enough with the moon at the full. Terror is tired after being ridden all day, so he won't gallop for long. Why don't you lean back and try to get some sleep whilst you can?'

120

She agreed and curled up in the corner. The last thing she expected to do was to sleep, yet she must have done. She was vaguely aware of the movement of the coach, of the passage of time, but could not have said how long they had been travelling when at last the coach began to slow down. She stirred and yawned, patting her mouth with her hand the way she had so often seen Mathilda do.

'Have we arrived yet?' she asked sleepily. 'Can you see your horse?'

'Vanessa gave me the name of an inn . . . I can hardly make out the sign in this light, but I think . . .' the coach lurched, then stopped. 'Yes, we've arrived.'

Jerome opened the door and jumped down. He said, his voice low and urgent, 'Stay there for a moment, whilst I make sure Vanessa is here.'

She saw him cross the courtyard and softly knock; the door opened. He slipped inside, was gone no more than thirty seconds, then reappeared, holding a lighted lantern.

'Yes, she's arrived. Out with you, Mathilda, and we'll confront the minx together! I'm sure she didn't realise what a pickle she was placing us in!'

It all sounded so feasible, Vanessa reflected as she crossed the yard, that had she not been Vanessa herself, she might easily have been completely taken in. As it was, he took her hand in a light clasp and led her into a small, square hall, then gestured towards the stairs.

'Quietly, my dear, we don't want to awaken the whole house. Vanessa is in the first bedroom on the right of the landing, and I think it best that we confront her together.'

She hung back a little, looking round uneasily.

'Why must we go upstairs? Why cannot we ring for a servant and get Vanessa to come down to us?'

'Because the servants, save for the one who let me in, are all abed! Come along, now.'

But by now, Vanessa was convinced that even Mathilda would have begun to suspect. She hung back, saying suspiciously, 'Where is the servant who let you in? Why has he disappeared? You go up, Jerome! I . . . I wish I'd never come with you!'

He had been holding her hand but now his arm encircled her waist. Strong as a band of steel, it urged her upwards.

'No more fuss, Mathilda. You'll accompany me, if you please. And don't, I beg you, begin to scream or cry out! The proprietress is an accommodating soul if well paid, and I've paid her well!'

It needed no effort now for Vanessa to sound frightened. She *was* afraid. What was this place and why had Jerome brought her here?

'No, no, I won't go,' she panted, grabbing at the banister rail. But he tore her fingers from the wood and manhandled her up the stairs and through the open door of a bedchamber leading off the small upper landing.

Inside the room, a fire burned. There was wine in a jug, standing on a table by the fire with two glasses near at hand. The bed was curtained with pale pink silk, there were lighted candles on the mantel, and the floor was covered with soft, pink carpet. Insensibly, it comforted her. A hideous vision of being raped in a garret receded a little. Raped first and then murdered, when Jerome discovered her identity, she thought wryly.

Jerome locked the door behind them, strode across the room, and began to pour wine into the glasses.

'My dear . . . my very dear Mathilda! I wanted to ask you to marry me in the conventional fashion, but, alas, I became increasingly convinced that you'd not have me! This way, my dear little girl, you'll find it much the best thing to accept my suit, and of course your Papa will be glad to marry you to me. I deeply regret it if I've frightened you, but unless you will swear on the bible to marry me forthwith, I can see I shall have to seduce you as well! The choice is yours, my dear! Now take off . . .'

He was advancing towards her, his eyes laughing but his mouth determined. She pushed back the hood of her cloak and faced him in the full candlelight, waiting. She wanted to close her eyes but the lids refused to obey her and her bright, terrified gaze remained fixed on him, like a rabbit mesmerised by a snake.

As she watched, recognition dawned; and fury. She had never in her life seen anyone angrier.

'You? *You?* What devil's work is this? How . . .'

He crossed the space between them and ripped off her cloak as though it had been made of paper. Then he rumpled her hair viciously until the powder had clouded out and dispersed. His hands were hard on her shoulders, pushing her into the chair. She flinched, sensing how he longed to hit her, but he only said between clenched teeth, 'Sit down!'

She sat down and he slumped into the chair opposite. For a moment he just looked at her, his eyes ice-cold, his face white under the tan. She felt a faint stirring of pity. He looked so tired and desperate!

'Well?'

He barked the monosyllable at her, and she knew that he was still very angry. She was afraid, and toyed for a minute with some conventional lie which would get her out of here without any more distress, but it would not do. It must be the truth.

'I lied about changing rooms with Matty.'

Her voice sounded very small and defiant.

'So I gather. Why?'

'I guessed you meant to do something like this, and I couldn't let you! Mathilda's my friend, you see.'

He nodded, then reached out and picked up one glass of wine. He handed it to her, then took the other and drained it at one draught.

'Why didn't you warn her? Put her on her guard against me?'

'She might not have believed me.' Vanessa sipped the wine and warmth curled down into her stomach, giving her courage. 'But if I had, she'd have ruined you, Jerome.'

'You mean she would have told everyone and disgraced me?'

'Yes.'

'Then why didn't you do it?'

She lowered her eyes. 'I couldn't. After all, you didn't ruin *me*, the night we stopped at the first inn, and . . .'

'And I could have done so, with one hand tied behind me. And with your blessing, because you didn't know very much, did you?'

The light was back in his eyes again now, but it was not a pleasant light. She felt fear stir, hot and choking, and moved uneasily in her chair, then sipped again at her wine.

'No, I didn't know much. Jerome, were you just abducting Matty for her money?'

He nodded carelessly, then got up and poured himself more wine. This time he kept the bottle by his side instead of replacing it on the table.

'Yes. I need that money. My estate is . . . but what does it matter, now? I suppose you took her place so that I'd be forced to marry you?'

She was so surprised that she sat bolt upright, spilling wine onto her pale green skirt.

'Goodness no, the thought never crossed my mind! Anyway, I've laid my plans so neatly that there will be no scandal. When Mathilda wakes up she'll read my note and know that everything is respectable and above board. But of course we must return to the inn as soon as possible. What's the time?'

He drained his wineglass, then consulted his watch.

'Nearly seven o'clock. Why?'

'As late as that? Well, we'd better set out at once!'

She half rose to her feet but he gestured her back to her chair and then, when she did not immediately obey him, he stood up and pushed her onto her seat once more.

'No use. We took over two hours to get here, and . . . but tell me what you said in your note.'

He poured himself more wine and she wished, uneasily, that he would stop drinking. She was sure, now, that he had planned not just to abduct her friend but to seduce her as well and this for some reason made him seem less the Jerome she knew and more unpredictable; dangerous, even.

'Well, I said that I'd recollected an old nurse of mine lived nearby and I'd borrowed Terror and gone to visit her. Then I wrote a second note which I gave to the boy who serves the drinks. I signed it with your name and just said you'd gone after me, because Terror was no lady's mount. Good, wasn't it?'

'Not bad. You thought I'd ride Terror, of course, instead of travelling in the coach. But I'm afraid it won't fadge, my little one! I left a note as well.'

Her eyes widened. 'Oh, no! I thought you'd

just leave me to . . . to. . . . But in any event, there will be no me to read your note so that won't matter!'

He laughed mirthlessly, and poured more wine into his glass. 'But I didn't send only you a note, my child!' He sipped reflectively at the liquid, looking at her over the brimming glass. 'I sent a note to my Mama as well, who is staying at the inn we passed yesterday called . . .'

'Tabor House; I saw you coming out of the stables,' Vanessa said in a hollow voice.

'Yes, that's the one. I begged my Mama to go at once to The Grapes Inn, arriving if possible by eight of the clock, to chaperon a young lady she would find there, possibly in some distress. I told her that I was intent upon compromising an heiress, and would look for her help and support in the matter.' He laughed suddenly. 'My God, but Demetria will never let me live this down! To abduct the wrong girl! To seduce the penniless Miss Norris instead of the rich Miss Randolph, because I failed to allow for the confounded interference of a silly little chit!'

'But . . . but you're not seducing the wrong girl,' Vanessa stammered. 'Truly, Jerome, it will be all right! Your Mama will read the note, I suppose, and go to the Grapes, but she'll realise at once that something's gone wrong, as soon as she finds herself confronting Miss Randolph.'

'That's rich, damme if it isn't! She's never met Miss Randolph, you little fool! She's an impetuous woman, Demetria, and she'll burst into that inn, wailing and lamenting that she's come to save Miss Randolph from a fate worse than death! That way, my child, she will establish once and for all that Miss Randolph has been abducted and almost certainly seduced, whilst loudly proclaiming her own innocence! Oh yes, that's how Demetria will handle the situation. I never doubted it for an instant, that was why I sent her the note!'

'Then we must leave at once, and stop her reaching the inn,' Vanessa cried, jumping to her feet.

This time, Jerome made no attempt to stop her but lounged to his feet too, looked her measuringly up and down, then grabbed hold of her, pulling her so close against him that she could feel his heartbeats thundering through her until her body seemed to throb with his emotions.

'It's too late, I tell you. The fat's in the fire and my goose is cooked. And so, incidentally, is yours! I certainly shan't marry you, but . . .'

He bent his head and covered her mouth with his. It was less a kiss than an attack and she cried out against his lips but he ignored her, working on her mouth until he forced it open, then deepening his kisses, at the same time undoing the fastenings of her gown so that presently she felt his fingers on her bare flesh and tried to cry out, but the sound was muffled by his mouth.

As suddenly as he had attacked her, it seemed, he released her. As their bodies parted he ripped

128

savagely at her gown, bringing it down to her waist. She tried to cover her bare breasts with her hands and he reached up and tugged her hair loose so that it tumbled down about her shoulders. She was weeping, the tears chasing themselves down her pale cheeks, her mouth swollen by his kisses, her flesh aching from his cruel grip.

'Get on the bed!'

'What . . .what?'

His hands were at his waist, unfastening the leather belt he wore. She cringed back, dragging her dress over her nakedness, sobs almost choking her. Was he going to beat her? She looked wildly round the room, searching for something to defend herself with or a means of escape. There was nothing. The door was locked and he was between her and the rest of the room. Her back was to the wall, the bed pressed against her left leg. Nothing else. No escape.

He threw his belt to the floor and began to pull off his shirt. She knew, then, what he meant to do. He had brought her here to seduce her and he would do just that, even though she was the wrong woman. He would do it to punish her for losing him the heiress!

He began to advance towards her, and there was a red light in his eyes she had never seen before. Her heart was hammering so loudly that her voice sounded tiny when she spoke.

'No. No, Jerome! *Please!*'

He was close now, his eyes narrowed, one curl escaping to hang over his forehead. She could see beads of sweat on his cheekbones and upper lip. She was deathly afraid.

'Yes. Yes, Jerome. Please! You'll say that presently, you pretty, foolish child!'

His hands closed on her shoulders. Irresistible in their strength. He pushed her slowly down onto the bed.

CHAPTER SEVEN

Curly had been puzzled but obedient when at last he realised that his mistress — nay, his goddess — really meant what she said; that he was to remain with Mathilda of the high voice and restless jerky movements until morning.

He was not happy, therefore, but he was determined to do as he had been told. And indeed, had his goddess only remained in her own room, he would have been as good as gold all night.

But she did not. When it was darkest there came soft footsteps, padding along the corridor. Curly whined softly to himself. It was the nice, large man who had spread soothing unguents upon his sores and whose voice always went gentle when he spoke to Curly's goddess.

He hesitated outside the door and Curly's tail stirred. A visitor? Should he, perhaps, bark a little? But in his adventurous and roaming existence the idea of guarding anything, warning anyone, had never been put into his head. So he merely sat up and faced the door, ready at the creak of the latch to bounce down onto the floor, tail going nineteen-to-the-dozen, mouth grinning with joy.

Unfortunately, the latch, when it eventually creaked, proved to belong to the door opposite and not to his door. He heard his goddess speak, then the other, then the door closed softly and the large man padded off down the hallway again.

There ensued a short pause, and during this Curly dozed a little, though he continued to sit up and face the door. He was uneasy; something was happening, but he did not know what. When his goddess opened her door, however, and stole out, closing it softly behind her, he came fully awake again.

He heard her descend the stairs, then cross the hall below. Whispers. With ears cocked right forward he strained to understand what was happening. The big front door swung open, was closed softly. He ran to the door and pressed his nose passionately against the crack, sniffing noisily. Yes, he could smell the fresh night air! She had gone! Forgotten him! Abandoned him!

Curly scratched the stout oak panels of the door, but the door did not give an inch. Frantically, he bounced back onto Mathilda's inanimate form, whining shrilly through his nose. Mathilda did not move but her even breathing jerked once or twice before becoming steady once more.

What must he do? Off the bed again, over to

the door, sniff deeply, scratch wildly, bounce back onto the bed again. This time, emboldened by the fact that Mathilda stirred, he barked. She muttered something. He barked again. Hopefully, she would wake and realise that something was very wrong.

But to his disappointment, a second and third bark only made her retreat beneath the blankets, heaving them up over her head and kicking out so vigorously that he was tipped ignominiously onto the floor.

But now his blood was up. She would wake if he had to drag the covers off her! He leapt onto the bed and began a vigorous excavation, digging with his strong front claws, barking, doing his utmost to rouse her. She fought back bravely, he had to admit that, kicking, pushing, keeping the blankets over her head.

But he won, in the end. She shouted at him, then climbed out of bed, shouting at him again when he jumped up at her and barked his admiration for her good sense. Though it had taken long enough!

She opened the door and he rocketed into the corridor, then glanced back. Come along, we'll catch them if we hurry! But the stupid female had gone back into her room, slamming the door crossly behind her. He did not hesitate this time, but fairly flew down the stairs, his bandaged leg a little stiff perhaps, but still responding well. The front door was shut. He circled the hall, sniffing hard at all the doors, but each was closed and he could tell that the rooms beyond were empty.

He tore back up the stairs, reached her door, and began to scratch and whine. She called out something in a cross and peevish voice: it sounded like 'do it against the stairs,' but that seemed to make no sense at all! He began to bark, desperate to get her help. Surely, surely the stupid female must come to her senses sooner or later and let him out, to pursue his goddess?

In the end, popular opinion brought Mathilda, furious and still swollen-eyed with sleep, out of her bedchamber. Other would-be sleepers were stirring, calling out, cursing the damned dog. Blearily, she opened her door and stood staring down at Curly. For a moment the dog gazed back, then rushed over to Vanessa's door and breathed noisily against it.

An evil thought entered Mathilda's head. It was, after all, far more Vanessa's affair than hers if the dog woke everyone on the landing! Very quietly, she opened the door, a little surprised to find it neither locked nor bolted, but then of course the maid would be coming to wake them early in the morning. She whispered 'In you go!' and tried to push the dog through the opening. He resisted for a moment, then suddenly bounced through, barked twice, deafening, and came straight out again, staring at her, Mathilda thought, as if it was she who had lost her senses, and not himself!

She was about to pursue him again and push him forcibly into the room when something about the room struck her. It seemed — empty! Vanessa had not spoken when the dog barked, had not stirred, even.

Before leaving her room, Mathilda had lit a candle from the embers of the fire. Now, she swung the light to illuminate her friend's bed. It was empty!

For the first time, Mathilda looked at Curly with respect. The dog had known! But what on earth could Vanessa be doing at this time of night? Curly, having made his point, ran down the stairs again, sniffed hard against the front door, pelted back up. But Mathilda was right in Vanessa's room now, searching for some clue as to her friend's disappearance. Her clothes had gone, and her boots. Her small bag remained. Frowning, Mathilda swung round to put the candlestick down upon the mantel whilst she investigated further — and there was a letter, with her name upon it, in the handwriting which she remembered so well from Vanessa's schoolbooks.

She snatched it down, tore the seal, and perused it eagerly. Then, very slowly, she picked up the candlestick and returned to her own room with it. He pushed at her fire with a stick of wood from the log box, then sank down on the chair, settled herself and re-read the letter.

'Dear Mathilda,' it ran. 'Don't worry because I'm not in my room, I decided since it was a clear morning that I'd visit a nurse of mine who only lives a few miles further down the road. I've taken Terror; he's had a good rest overnight, so will be up to the

135

short ride. I'll be back soon after breakfast. Van.'

Having read it again, she was just as baffled as she had been the first time. It simply did not make sense! How could Vanessa say it was a clear morning? It was still pitch dark outside, far too dark to go visiting old nurses! And besides, on *horseback?* She was in her green gown, and Terror had an ordinary saddle! To attempt to ride him without a sidesaddle, when clad in a fairly voluminous skirt, would be idiotic!

Abruptly making up her mind, she jumped to her feet, taking Curly by surprise, for he had been sitting watching her face intently as though to read her expression.

'I'll go and wake Jerome,' she said aloud. 'He would be most annoyed if I did not!' Curly, leaping to his feet, gave a little yap of encouragement. 'Get out from under my feet, you foolish animal! Now I wonder where Jerome sleeps?'

Perhaps fortunately, the noise of Curly's frequent rushes downstairs, his skirmish with Mathilda and his shrill barks had woken the chambermaid, who now appeared on the attic stairs, her hair in curl papers, a candle wavering in one hand.

'What's 'appened?' she quavered. 'Is it robbers, Miss?'

'No. Merely that I find myself unable to look after this dog and wish to give him back to his master,' Mathilda said with all the aplomb at her command. Her hand strayed to her own curl papers, forgotten in the excitement, and she began to untie them and drop them absently into the pocket of her wrap.

'Oh, I see, Miss.' The girl began to retreat up the stairs again and Mathilda had to call her back.

'Here a minute!'

'Oh, I'm sorry, Miss, I thought . . .'

'My dear child,' Mathilda said patiently, 'I do not know in which room Mr Harcourt sleeps. Perhaps you can advise me?'

'Mr 'arcourt. Is 'e the lovely tall gent wiv the black 'air?'

'Yes,' Mathilda said, not mincing matters. 'Which room?'

'Door at the far end of the corridor. G'night, Miss.'

It took Mathilda a little while to make herself presentable enough to wake Jerome. She had to take out all her curl papers, brush her hair, wash her face and press a cold-water flannel on her still sleepy eyes, and finally, put on her velvet slippers. Then, candlestick in hand, she set out along the corridor to his room.

She knocked, then called quietly, then after Curly had almost elbowed her aside to inhale with a noise like a hurricane against the door jamb, she opened the door gently.

She lifted her candle and the light fell upon another empty bed!

At this point, Curly completely forgot his manners. He had, it seemed, run out of patience. Seizing the hem of her wrap in his mouth, he tugged her down the stairs, across the hall, and up to the front door. There he stood, eyeing her, whining and wagging his tail, his eyes almost speaking with their eloquence.

She struggled with the latch and the door creaked open. Like a flash of lightning, the dog whipped through it and was gone, into the darkness. The moon was waning as dawn approached and there was a line of pale grey on the horizon. She could just see Curly's white coat whipping round the corner and out of sight. She called to him in a small voice. It looked so big and dark out there! She had no desire to venture out after the dog!

She waited a few moments, then returned indoors and shut the oak door behind her. She did not slide the bolt across though, in case Jerome, or Vanessa, or both returned and desired admittance. As for Curly, he could howl outside if he wished, but he was not entering her room again for what was left of the night!

Vanessa felt the bed give as Jerome pinned her to the mattress with his weight, holding her gripped tight so that she could not struggle. He tugged her gown down to her waist and began to kiss her. Gently at first, his mouth travelled over her eyelids, her cheeks, the side of her neck. He began to kiss the soft white skin of her breasts, murmuring that she was beautiful, honey-sweet, that she must not fight him for she would enjoy love when it came. She was a woman, soft, supple, tender-fleshed, and women were fashioned for love.

Then, suddenly, he stopped talking and his mouth was cruel on her, hot, hard kisses turned her white skin rosy, and made her twist and whimper in his grasp. Yet he was disturbing her terribly with the change from tenderness to harshness, from love to lust, making her doubt her wish to escape.

The air was cool on her suddenly, and his face was above hers, his eyes still glowing with frightening fire. Then he kissed her lips, coolly and deliberately and for a moment there was magic between them. The kiss continued, gentle, exploratory, and she knew that she loved him, that he was not going to force her against her will.

When his kiss changed, becoming fierce, demanding, she no longer drew back. Her own desire, so subtly roused, rose to meet his so that he no longer held her down but stroked her, letting one hand fondle her small breast until the nipple hardened in his fingers, signalling her desire, proving to his experienced mind and body that her defiance had all but fled.

He moved his weight off her, sure of her now. She would be his, and willingly. Revenge was forgotten in the heat of his desire for her. He wanted her so! Gently, he pushed her gown down round her hips, seeing her smooth, silky body with its childishly slender waist, its womanly curves. He touched her almost wonderingly; she was so young and sweet, so innocent, yet she had temper, and plenty of spirit; she would make a wonderful lie-beside, he could scarcely wait to take her!

Beneath his gaze the big green eyes opened and looked straight up into his face. She looked very serious, very young.

'Jerome? I love you.'

It should have been a signal for him to continue his lovemaking, yet the quiet words stopped him dead in his tracks.

'If you loved me, it would be all right. But you don't. And I don't want to end up hating you, and myself.'

He was completely taken back. He stared at her, then smiled mockingly.

'You won't hate me! You'll enjoy it . . . you are enjoying it!'

She shook her head; a tiny negative movement.

'You are!' he persisted. 'Believe me, I can tell!'

'It isn't that, Jerome. It's revenge, isn't it? You don't want me in the right sort of way, you just want a woman, and it's for that I could never forgive you. Nor forgive myself.'

His eyes strayed over her naked body, marked by his hands, his mouth. She was his for the taking, she could never stop him now, even if she wanted to! Just looking at her brought him to a pitch of lust he had seldom experienced. He *must* have her! She was only a woman, she would forget hatred and self-disgust once she was his!

He looked into her eyes, and saw they were full of tears. But she would not let them fall, would not let weeping stay his hand. Damn it, she was a brave little soul. She had done him no harm, she had only saved her friend from his plottings. All that talk of love — what *was* love? If he loved anyone in the world beside himself it was this little red-haired scrap of womanhood who lay beneath him and defied him still!

He knew, then, that her danger was over. Clumsily, he pulled up her gown to cover her breasts, then got out of bed and fetched her a glass of wine. She was shuddering and trembling so hard that the bed shook and he teased her, wrapped her in a blanket, swore he had never meant to scare her so — it had been the wine, and his damned temper.

The tears spilled over at that, as he knew they must, so he put his arms round her and comforted her as he had done before, murmuring childish endearments against her hair. All the time he could feel this strange, tender emotion that he had never felt before growing deeper and stronger so that he thought his heart must burst if he did not tell her how he felt, but he knew he must not let a word pass his lips. He could not possibly marry a penniless chit, no matter how his heart longed for her, and she was far from the type of female one made one's mistress! They would have to part. No need to make it more difficult for her by admitting that he loved her too, loved her more with each passing minute.

And presently, when she was calm, he suggested that they should make themselves respectable and then order a conveyance to take them speedily back to the Grapes.

'After all, miracles do happen,' he said as they took turns at the washbasin. 'My dear Mama may have managed to hold her tongue!'

Mathilda had barely fallen asleep, it seemed, before the chambermaid was swishing back the curtains, remarking brightly that it was as pleasant and sunny a spring day as one could wish for.

'Well, that's something to be thankful for,' Mathilda said a little snappishly. 'Dear me, what I've suffered! Have you woken Miss Norris yet?'

'Not yet, Miss. I'm going over to her room next, with this note and her breakfast tray.' The girl showed Mathilda a folded slip of paper. 'Now eat your nice breakfast whilst it's hot.'

It was a good breakfast; Mathilda's mouth fairly watered at the sight of the pot of hot chocolate, the newly baked bread rolls, the pats of butter and the jar of orange marmalade. But it watered more at the sight of the letter in the maid's hand. How she longed to know what was inside it!

'If Miss isn't in her room, perhaps you would bring the letter to me,' she said casually, however, pouring her chocolate. 'I'll see that it's delivered to her.'

'Well, no one's up and about yet, Miss, it being early still,' the maid said doubtfully. 'But I'll go and give her door a tap.'

Two minutes later she was back in Mathilda's room, round-eyed.

'She's gone out, Miss, sure enough! Wanted to

enjoy the sunshine, I daresay, and the little dog with her. I'll give you the letter then, if I may.'

Mathilda took the paper, waited with her fingers twitching whilst the girl ambled out of the room, then slit the seal with her butter knife and eagerly read the note, which was signed 'Jerome'.

'*Have been called away on urgent business,*' it read. '*Don't be alarmed, for I've arranged for Demetria to rescue you, and carry you to London in my stead. All will end well, I promise, and think of your Duke!*'

Mathilda sat and frowned over this extraordinary epistle whilst the chocolate cooled in her cup. The more she thought, the more mysterious the entire business seemed. Demetria? Who on earth was she? And why should she take Vanessa to London in Jerome's stead? Absently, she buttered a roll and spread it thickly with marmalade. It is I who was to take Vanessa to London, she thought suddenly, Jerome was merely accompanying us both. Escorting us, in fact.

From this thought, her mind continued on to another. Jerome had been paying court to her, and it had been fun to flirt with him, try to keep his interest, behave a little more daringly than she would have cared to do under her godparents' roof. But it had occurred to her a couple of times that though he seemed to take little or no notice of Vanessa, and though Vanessa seemed positively to dislike him, there had been something between them.

Nothing romantic, no gay flirtation to while away the dull hours spent in the inn. No exchange of soft glances, no squeezing of fingers, no hand held a fraction longer than necessary.

She frowned. Yet there *had* been something. She knew herself to be a practical young woman, not given to flights of fancy, yet she had noticed *something* . . .

Her train of thought was interrupted by a hurried tap at the door which opened to admit the chambermaid, accompanied by the ubiquitous Curly.

'The lady's little dawg, Miss. He's in a state, looks as if he's run miles.'

'Take him away!' Mathilda said sharply. 'I won't have him in here like that! Tell the stable lad to clean him up and bandage his leg again, and to keep him shut in, for goodness sake. I'll . . . I'll see to him later.' She paused, uncertain how to frame the next question, then decided that there was no tactful way of putting it.

'Has Mr Harcourt returned to the inn yet? Or Miss Norris?'

The girl's rather protuberant eyes almost fell out onto her round and rosy cheeks.

'Oh, Miss, have they run off together? We did wonder . . . Well, and her such a nice young thing, too! How could she leave her little dawg, though, and she so fond of it! Well, I . . .'

'No, no, of course they haven't run off together,' Mathilda said desperately. 'How foolish you are! The note explains all! Miss Norris very

144

naughtily left the inn early, to go and visit her elderly nurse, who lives in these parts. She left a note for Mr Harcourt, explaining what she had done, and he's gone in search of her. She went off on his stallion, you see, and the animal is not a lady's mount.'

'Oh, I *see*,' the girl said, her colour deepening. 'I'm sorry, Miss I'm sure, if I thought wrong of your friend, but . . .'

'Never mind, never mind,' Mathilda said hastily. 'Now, can you help me into my clothes, since my friend isn't here to assist me?'

The maid thought that she could be spared for a few moments, and with her willing if inexpert help, Mathilda was dressed and ready to face the day in no more than half an hour.

Her first action upon going downstairs was to visit the coffee room, half-expecting to find another note propped up on the mantel, probably explaining away the two previous epistles, but there was nothing, and no one seemed particularly interested in her so she concluded that the chambermaid had already spread the story (whether fiction or not she had not the faintest idea) of Vanessa's elderly nurse.

Her next action was to repair to the stable to find out when the coach would be ready to continue on its journey to London. She had no objection to waiting another hour or so, but it was becoming increasingly clear to her that whatever had happened, she must begin to formulate her own plans for the rest of the journey.

Vanessa's note had promised a speedy return, Jerome's had mentioned an unknown female, but so far only Curly had put in an appearance, looking as if he had been searching the surrounding countryside all night, and that was not much use!

She went to the stable and spoke to the head groom, who seemed unnaturally perplexed.

'But Miss, the coach went hours since! I dunno what time 'xactly but before daylight! There'll be a stage along in an hour heading for the capital, but your coach went!'

'I suppose Terror must have been too much for Vanessa, so she ordered up the coach,' Mathilda said aloud. 'And then Jerome must have pursued her on Terror.'

The man looked at her as though she had taken leave of her senses.

'Oh no, Miss! Why, Mr. 'arcourt took the coach, not the young lady.'

'I see. In that case, Miss Norris must have ridden Terror as she threatened. Dear me, I do hope no harm has come to her!'

'No indeed, Miss. 'Cept the black stallion wot Mr 'arcourt rode yesterday's in 'is stall, quiet as a lamb.'

'Wha-at?' Mathilda shrieked. 'Then who . . . what . . . ?'

It was at this point that a dashing conveyance came round the corner and drew up in the stableyard. The window of the coach was let down with a clatter and a woman leaned out. She was not in the first flush of youth but she had night black hair, dark, dramatic eyes, and a passionate mouth. She reminded Mathilda vaguely of someone.

'Hey! You!'

She spoke in a high imperious tone, the tone of one accustomed to being obeyed. The groom, though a man in middle age, sprang to the window of the coach, tugging his forelock.

'Yes, ma'am?'

'My son . . . has he left this inn? His name is Mr Harcourt, and . . .'

'Why yes, ma'am, he's left. With a young lady, this young lady's friend.'

The dark eyes skimmed Mathilda, then dismissed her.

'I see. Where were they bound?'

Mathilda felt her indignation rise to boiling pitch. She had been longing to quarrel with someone ever since she had awoken to find herself deserted and still, metaphorically speaking, in the dark. But now, with the groom's last words, light flashed blindingly upon her. So that was it!

'Your son, ma'am, left no message as to his eventual destination. But since he has without a doubt abducted my friend, I assume they'll be heading for the border.'

Demetria hissed in her breath and laid one hand dramatically over her heart.

'Abduction? My son? Oh never, never! He must be deep in love, and . . .'

'And as soon as he discovered she was a very wealthy heiress, he found he could not live without her,' Mathilda finished sarcastically.

'I cannot allow . . .'

'My dear ma'am, there is very little either of us can do! I would give a great deal to be able to help my friend, for the poor little soul is innocent, and very vulnerable. She has no parents, only a guardian, and will be quite unable to defend herself against your son's practised seduction.'

'My son . . .'

'Is quite fifteen years older than his victim, and a great deal more experienced. I will put it no stronger than that. And now you must excuse me if you please, for a friend will be here shortly, to accompany me to the capital.'

Mathilda turned on her heel and stalked indignantly into the inn. She went up to her room, finished her packing, and then came down to the coffee room, ordered a pot of coffee and some macaroons and asked the landlord, who was serving some customers, whether anyone had been enquiring for her.

'Not a soul, Miss. But you was talking to a lady out in the stableyard, earlier . . .'

'That was Mrs Harcourt. I am waiting for . . . well, for someone else.'

'Oh, was that Demetria Harcourt?' the landlord asked with interest. 'A very sporting lady, I understand, and much talked about in polite circles, though . . . Why Miss, whatever is the matter?'

For Mathilda had turned on her heel and rushed from the room. She burst into her bed-chamber, threw herself on the bed, and began to pummel the pillows and bite the bedding with temper, finally rolling over on her back and going off into gales of laughter.

Curly, who had followed her upstairs, sat, head cocked, and watched her with interest. Funny woman!

'Demetria Harcourt! Of course, Jerome *would* call his mother by her first name. So that was who she reminded me of! Oh dear oh dear, this wretched business is rapidly turning into one of Mr Sheridan's more stupid comedies! Now I must pull myself together and catch the very next stage to the metropolis. And won't I give Jerome a piece of my mind when he arrives in Hanover Square!'

But whilst she packed, she was forced to con-clude that for Vanessa, this was real tragedy. She had no idea how Jerome had found out that Vanessa was Miss Bascombe, but she was sure that he had done so. Poor Van didn't even *like* the fellow, and she was alone in his clutches. But think though she might, there seemed no way in which she could help. If he had not . . . her mind winced away from the word and she rephrased the thought. If Vanessa was still a virtuous maid, then the affair could be covered up, some story con-cocted.

With this in mind, she rang for the maid to carry her bags downstairs and determined, upon

149

her arrival in London, to beg Lady Remington to assist her young friend.

Demetria sank back upon the soft leather squabs of her coach and felt waves of elation and relief engulf her. The comfort of acquiring a rich daughter-in-law, by whatever dubious means! Now, the terrible suspicion that she might be forced to agree to a marriage of convenience between herself and the rich but depraved Lord Forsythe, merely in order to be able to command the elegancies of life, receded. Lord Forsythe's taste ran to very young damsels of the servant-girl variety, and he wanted a wife to give a thin veneer of respectability to his sordid little *affaires*. She was neither a kind nor an imaginative woman, but she had not relished turning a blind eye to the distress of such innocent young damsels as came Forsythe's way, nor of the veiled disgust with which the Beau Monde would regard her.

She scarcely spared a thought, however, for the young girl caught in her son's toils. If she had considered her, she would merely have thought her a fortunate creature to be seduced by a man as young and handsome as Jerome. Demetria was a realist. She had been married at seventeen to an elderly widower, who had bedded her with goatlike thoroughness solely in order to beget heirs. Once she had borne him two sons she took lovers and discovered that there could be pleasure for both in a mating. But love was merely a word, to whose meaning she was a stranger, so she certainly did not expect Jerome to marry for love, whatever she might pretend.

Presently, she took out her son's note and read it again, frowning. He said nothing about a flight to the border nor, indeed, did he mention marriage, save to remark that this action would ensure Mr Randolph's compliance with such a course.

She smiled, and rapped sharply on the roof of the coach with her parasol. He had asked her to proceed to Hanover Square, and to take with her the young chit who had spoken so rudely to her in the inn-yard. No doubt he had taken one of his fancies to the blonde piece, but he had behaved like a dutiful son and abducted the heiress, no doubt plain, as they usually were. And upon consideration, she realised that her own presence in the capital might well be necessary to his plans. Yes, if the story of his abduction could be hushed up so that no one knew the truth except the interested parties, then Jerome would doubtless deliver Miss Randolph to her own charge, in Hanover Square. Then he and Sir Thomas could go straight to the distraught Papa, with the story of Jerome's infatuation and the news that he had left a willing Miss Randolph in the care of his own mother. It would then merely be a matter of arranging the marriage with the least delay, and without giving the scandalmongers food for gossip. All could be made tidy, and it would simply appear that the heiress had fallen for Jerome's undoubted charms.

In response to her knocking the coach slowed, then stopped, and the coachman's ruddy visage appeared at the window.

'Yes, Ma'am?'

'Drive straight to Sir Thomas Remington's house in Hanover Square, if you please.'

'Very good, ma'am.'

The coach sagged to one side as the man heaved his considerable bulk back into his seat, then proceeded on its way.

'Mathilda . . . I mean Miss Randolph's *gone?* But . . . but we said to wait . . . I said to wait . . .' stammered Vanessa. For once, her calm had entirely deserted her. '*Where* has she gone? Is she . . . has she . . .'

Jerome, who had followed her into the hall, took hold of her arm in a steadying grasp.

'Steady, my . . . steady, Miss Norris,' he murmured. 'Don't worry, Miss Randolph has a head on her shoulders and won't come to harm.' He turned to the innkeeper. 'Miss Norris went off early this morning to find an elderly acquaintance, and I set out in search of her. We did leave notes for Miss . . . er Miss Randolph, telling her . . .'

'I'm sure, sir. Miss Randolph did wait for a while, and then a lady arrived — Mrs Demetria Harcourt, it was — and shortly after speaking to her, the young lady announced she wished to catch the next stage to London.' He coughed deprecatingly, glancing slyly at Jerome. 'But despite my telling her, sir, she would take the slow!

152

I doubt she'll be in the capital until mid-afternoon at the earliest.'

'I see. Then we had best set out ourselves.'

Jerome swung round on his heel, his mouth set, but once outside Vanessa tugged at his arm.

'Don't look so cross, Jerome,' she begged. 'I think it sounds as though your Mama and Mathilda merely exchanged a few words and then parted. Probably no harm has been done. After all, if she knew the true story, surely Mathilda would have gone with your Mama to London? She would have got there by now, or very nearly.'

Jerome snorted. 'Much you know! Demetria travels so slowly that very likely she and the stage will reach the posting inn at the same time! Nevertheless, you do talk sense, sometimes. We'll go round and have a word with the groom; I have to get Terror now, at any rate.'

They repaired to the stableyard, where they found the groom all agog.

'Oh yes, sir, Mrs 'arcourt was 'ere, and in a state,' the young man told them eagerly. 'I didn't speak to 'er myself, bein' busy wi' groomin' the prads, but I couldn't 'elp but 'ear!'

'Well, man? What did you hear?'

'She's got a son, sir, what's bin a-stayin' 'ere. And 'e lit out last night, wiv a heiress!'

'Gracious,' Vanessa said mildly. 'What did the *young* lady say to that? Miss Randolph, the lady with the golden hair who left on the stage just now?'

'Didn't pay much attention to what she said,' the man admitted. 'But she flounced round on 'er 'eel and ran back into the inn.'

'I see. Well, Mr Harcourt, what shall we do now?'

The groom had been turning away but he spun round, his lower jaw dropping.

'Mr *'arcourt*? Oh sir, I never . . .'

'I'm sure you didn't,' Jerome said soothingly. 'Now would you kindly saddle and bridle my black stallion and have him ready for me to ride in, say, ten minutes? Miss Norris here will ride in the coach.'

'Not ten, twenty,' Vanessa contradicted firmly. 'I am parched and starving hungry and I daresay we'd both like to tidy ourselves.'

They went towards the inn, greeted the interested innkeeper with the news that the stable staff were even now rubbing down the coach horses and getting Mr Harcourt's stallion ready to leave, and ordered hot coffee and a plate of pasties.

Sitting down on the settle nearest the fire, Vanessa patted the cushion beside her.

'Sit down, Jerome, and let's talk this over! Now! I suppose you think that Mathilda knows all?'

Unexpectedly, Jerome shook his head. 'No. But she will, as soon as she gets to Hanover Square. I can guess what must have happened. Demetria arrived, so eager to Tell All that she probably neglected to say *who* her son had abducted! And Mathilda promptly leapt to the conclusion that I'd abducted you!'

'Well, you did,' Vanessa pointed out, reaching for the coffee pot.

'No, I . . . Well, not deliberately, at any rate! What we must do now is to reach London before the stage does so, and furthermore, reach Mathilda before she meets up with my dear Mama in Hanover Square, and is properly introduced.'

'I see. Well then, our next course of action seems very plain, to me.' She bit hungrily into a pasty and exclaimed thickly, 'I say, this is *good.*'

Jerome drained his coffee cup and got to his feet, prowling restlessly across to the window.

'Do hurry up, child, speed is essential! What is our next course of action, then? It doesn't seem very plain to me!'

'No, because men's minds are less elastic than females. We must get Mathilda off the stage, of course, before it reaches London.'

Jerome jumped. 'Get her off the stage? How simple! And yet since I've no idea where the coach will stop, more difficult than it appears. Come on, tell me the rest.'

'It will stop on the heath. If we . . . er . . . persuade it to do so.'

Jerome returned to the settle, sat down, and swung Vanessa round to face him. She continued to chew stolidly, but her eyes were full of dancing mischief.

'What on *earth* do you mean, you hell-born brat?'

155

Vanessa swallowed her mouthful, brushed crumbs off her lips, and sighed regretfully.

'That was delicious, Jerome. Do have one! What I mean is, let's hold them up!'

Jerome reached absently for a pasty then stopped, with the pie halfway to his mouth.

'Hold them up? You really *have* run mad! Masked, of course, and with guns!'

Vanessa nodded. 'Of course. I've got my cousin's clothes upstairs, and we can wind mufflers round our faces and pull our hats right down over our eyes. I've not got a gun, of course, but I can use a bit of stick. If I keep it half under my cloak no one will guess.'

Jerome's strong white teeth bit into the pasty. He said through his mouthful, 'It's quite mad! Why should anyone want to hold up a stage-coach, and the slow one, at that? Even if we did it successfully, and managed to get Mathilda off, what would we say to her?'

Vanessa considered. 'Well, we could hold her to ransom! Then you wouldn't have to marry her and she wouldn't have to be compromised by you. I'm sure she'd much prefer to part with a large sum of money, honestly!'

Jerome got to his feet, a scowl darkening his brow though his lips twitched.

'That is undoubtedly the biggest damned insult I've ever had to swallow! How do you know, brat, that being compromised by me isn't a most delightful experience? In fact I'll take leave to tell you that a great many ladies of my acquaintance have enjoyed it excessively!'

'Now stop boasting, Jerome, and be serious! Once we've got Mathilda off the coach we tell her the truth, of course! Well, no, not the *truth*, exactly, but the story we concocted earlier. That I ran away because I thought you were going to return me to Aunt . . . to my Aunt, and that you suspected I might do some such thing, dashed out of the inn and got into the coach with me.'

'And that we then broke a wheel and were stranded in a farmhouse until a replacement could be found,' sighed Jerome. 'If she'll believe that she'll believe anything! And *then* what?'

'Goodness, I can't live your life for you,' Vanessa said impatiently. 'Woo the girl, if you're so keen to marry her! I won't allow you to abduct her and don't you think of it, but if you behave, I'll never tell anyone what we did last night.'

He took her hands, pulling her to her feet, his dark eyes lit with laughter.

'What we did last night! You have less to tell than any other female I've bedded with!' He tucked her hand into his elbow, then led her outside into the hall. 'Go upstairs to your room — I take it they've not hired it out to anyone else? No? Good. Go up then, and change into your breeches and put your cap in the waistband. Then put your cloak on and we'll trust no one notices you're a hermaphrodite.'

'What? Herma . . . what?'

157

'Half lad, half lass. Go on, and don't be long. And Vanessa!'

She was halfway up the stairs but turned, brows raised.

'Yes?'

'You've changed! Why are you so gay and light-hearted?'

She smiled mockingly. 'Wouldn't you like to know! I'll be as quick as I can.'

She was as good as her word, and by the time she reached the stableyard Jerome was ready for her. He was mounted on Terror, who sidled and grabbed at his bit, eager to be off, and he held the lead-rein of a demure little dun mare with a lively eye and a white star on her forehead.

'Up with you, Van, and we'll go straight to the heath.'

They rode out of the yard, knees brushing as their heads leaned close.

'Did you bring your pistols, Jerome? Can I hold one?'

He grinned down at her, excitement lighting devils in his eyes.

'No, you can't; I'll wager you've never held a gun in your life! Just try to keep up with me, and when we reach the heath look out for a clump of trees to lurk behind whilst we wait for the stage. I'll do any shooting necessary, and it'll be over the horses' heads. *You'd* probably kill the leading horse!'

She chuckled, her eyes as bright as his.

'I would not, I'm very fond of horses!'

He dug his heels into Terror's sides and the big horse lengthened his stride. The dun mare kept pace, and they rode towards London knee to knee, like two comrades.

'Is that it?'

Vanessa leaned forward, tugging her cap down over her eyes and her muffler up over her mouth.

Jerome stared intently, then crouched in the saddle.

'It is, by God! Follow me!'

Taking his lead, Vanessa dug her heels into the dun mare and drew over so that their mounts thundered down upon the stage at a gallop, the dun's nose only inches behind Terror's. The coachman, seeing and hearing them, shouted to his horses to whoa and began to bawl contradictory instructions to his roof-passengers; sit tight, duck down, defend themselves. Naturally enough, he merely succeeded in creating a great deal of confusion.

The coach had been travelling slowly, but when Jerome's bullet had whistled past the driver's head and the coachman leaned back on the reins, the sudden shock of its stopping sent a crate of hens tipping over the side into the road, and brought the guard, who had manfully turned his ancient blunderbuss towards the horsemen, abruptly to his knees. The blunderbuss shot from his hands and disappeared into a nearby ditch. The guard, open-mouthed, sat down again, feeling that he, at any rate, was out of the running so far as driving the intruders off was concerned.

Meanwhile, the crate had burst on impact and the hens, only momentarily baffled by their freedom, spilled into the road and got to their feet, shouting murder and mayhem as hens will. After a wild glance round they set off, all ten of them, in ten different directions, cackling and flapping as if the devil himself was after them.

On the roof a man with a red face began to shout that 'them 'ens is prize 'ens,' and to extol the coach driver and guard to 'give us a 'and to cotch they!'

Vanessa slipped out of the saddle and approached the shouting, rocking coach, repressing a wild desire to burst out laughing. One glance at the baffled expression on Jerome's face as he strove to hold Terror still whilst pointing his pistols menacingly at the coach would, she reflected, have made a cat laugh.

She no sooner neared the coach, however, than a small white dog, tied to one of the outside seats, gave a yelp of excitement and launched himself over the side — to end up dangling like someone in a hangman's noose.

'Curly! Let that dog down!' shrieked Vanessa, completely forgetting to keep her voice low. Jerome, behind her, said gruffly, 'Someone cut that dog loose at once!'

The red-faced farmer, still bemoaning the loss of his prize hens, produced a clasp knife and slashed the rope so that the gasping, retching Curly could fall onto the carriageway. It said much for his recuperative powers that within thirty seconds he had staggered to his feet, uttered a feeble yelp, and tottered as close to his mistress as he could get. Vanessa bent down and scooped him up into her arms, suffering what was visible of her face to be thoroughly licked whilst Curly moaned with relief at having rediscovered his goddess.

Jerome, dismounting and with pistols held ready, threw open the coach door. Inside, his eyes flickered over a couple of fat farmers' wives, a weedy-looking clerk, a sailor, and finally, upon the patrician countenance of Miss Mathilda Randolph.

'You there! That your dawg?' rasped Jerome in what he hoped was an unrecognisable voice.

Heads were shaken.

'You, Miss! In the corner! That your dawg?'

'What if it is? Mathilda said coldly, 'It's no crime to own a dog.'

'Ho, but this dog's been *stole*,' Vanessa announced shrilly. 'You come wiv us, Miss, and do your 'splaining to the Constables.'

Mathilda was no fool. She had seen Curly's rapturous greeting of the 'highwaymen', and now saw a red curl peeping from beneath the smaller person's ragged cap.

'All right, but I just hope you've a good reason for this,' she said ominously, making the coachload of passengers, once the aggressors

161

were long gone, agree that she was a well-plucked 'un.

So Mathilda stepped down from the coach. Jerome threw her up onto Terror's saddle, mounted behind her, and gestured curtly to Vanessa to follow suit. In a moment they were out of earshot of the road and galloping towards the distant woods.

'Well?'

They were in the thick of the woods now and explanations could no longer be deferred. Jerome smiled ingratiatingly at the golden-haired beauty in the curve of his arm.

'Well, Mathilda, the long and short of it was that we had to get you off that confounded coach! You see . . .'

He proceeded with the fiction that he had pursued Vanessa, bound for her elderly nurse's home, had accompanied her there, arguing for a speedy return, but that the wheel had come off the coach.

'We were very much in hot water, but I recollected that my Mama was staying at an inn not far off, and begged her to go to the inn and carry you with her to Hanover Square. I cannot imagine why she did not do so!'

Mathilda's cheeks reddened.

'It was the notes! I was so confused! In fact, Jerome, I'm afraid I rather let your mother believe that you'd abducted poor Vanessa!'

His dark eyes narrowed with real anger, she

thought nervously.

'My God, how could you do such a thing? What about poor little Vanessa's reputation? Thank goodness we have her nurse to speak for us — and anyway, it was scarcely the middle of the night when you found us missing.'

'It was,' Mathilda said resentfully. 'At least, I didn't actually look at the time, but it was quite dark when Curly woke me, barking and yelping and jumping all over me. And then of course, I found Van's note . . .'

She did not notice Vanessa's guilty jump, nor how the colour flew to her cheeks.

'And then, when the girl brought my breakfast, there was *your* note,' Mathilda continued in an aggrieved tone. 'That confused me even . . .'

'But I didn't write you a note,' Jerome exclaimed. 'What on earth . . .'

'It wasn't to me, exactly,' Mathilda admitted, feeling a little awkward all of a sudden. 'It was *addressed* to Vanessa. But I didn't scruple to open it since she had disappeared and I hoped it might give me a clue to her whereabouts. But all it said was that someone called Demetria would be along presently, and would give Vanessa a lift to London! Now tell me what that meant!'

Jerome glanced wildly at Vanessa. 'You'd better explain,' he said gloomily.

Vanessa lowered her eyes demurely, but glanced wickedly up at him through her lashes.

'Oh, Jerome, it's so embarrassing! Must I tell?'

Wondering uneasily what wild idea his love had concocted this time, Jerome said sternly, 'Of course you must tell,' thinking that, since his own mind was a complete blank, almost any story would be better than none; infinitely better than the truth!

'Jerome's Mama is well acquainted with my Godmama, Lady Harrison, and Jerome thought it might look better if his Mama delivered me to her door, instead of himself. After all, his reputation . . .' she lowered her eyes again, then exclaimed 'Oh! There's a horrid *thing* on Curly's neck, all fat and grey and shiny, like a bead.'

'It's a tick,' Jerome said. 'I'll get it off later, with a lighted taper.'

'*Burn* it off? How horrible!' Vanessa shuddered. 'Well, shall we ride on now, into London?'

'Wait a minute,' Mathilda protested. 'What about *me*? If Mrs Harcourt was taking you to your Godmama's as a respectable chaperon, what was I supposed to do? Arrive with Jerome, and no reputation whatsoever?'

Jerome tutted gently. 'Really, Mathilda, what an unkind remark! I had naturally arranged for one of the girls from the inn to accompany us.'

'Oh, I see, I'm sorry,' Mathilda said, though she still looked a little suspicious. 'Just explain to me why . . .'

'I'll explain. Come over here for a minute.'

Vanessa led her friend a short distance from where Jerome stood, holding the reins of both horses, then whispered; 'He wanted to be alone

164

with you for a few moments, you goose! He wanted to ask you if there was a chance for him.'

'A chance?' Mathilda's eyes grew round with gratification. 'Well, if only I'd known! I like him very well, you know, and would like to know him better still. Of course, I want to enjoy my first Season but at the end of it, if we are both still of the same mind . . .'

'There! Well, I shall say nothing,' Vanessa assured her friend mendaciously. 'But just to know there's hope will mean a lot to him. Now let's ride in to London.'

But Mathilda hung back. 'Two of us on one horse? And you dressed as a boy? I declare I won't make such a spectacle of myself.'

They rejoined Jerome and Vanessa explained how Mathilda felt.

'So why should she not take my mount, and I'll wait here until you can return for me?' she suggested nobly, for the afternoon was rapidly drawing to its close.

'It's not to be thought of. But I do have a solution. Of sorts, that is.'

Both girls turned and surveyed Jerome with unwinking stares. Despite himself, he grinned at them, his teeth gleaming in the gathering grey of late afternoon.

'Don't look at me as if I might eat you! Look, Mathilda's been taken by highwaymen, right?'

Two heads, one gold, one burnished copper, nodded solemnly.

'Then she will have her purse taken, and be released, to make her way back into London as best she can. Or would have been, had we really been highwaymen. Right?'

Further nods, a little less certain.

'Then I suggest we wait here until it is really dark, and then ride quietly into London, by the back roads. Mathilda must ride with me, I fear, since we've no sidesaddle and she's blessed with that con . . . that pretty skirt. I shall take her right up to my Aunt's front door, and then let her down, whereupon she will knock and announce ringingly to the world at large that she was kidnapped and all her money taken, and that she's walked miles and miles.'

'Yes, that's a capital notion; and then you must faint,' Vanessa said, quite carried away by the idea. 'What about me, Jerome?'

'You? Oh, I'll take you to a respectable hotel where you may spend the night, and then tomorrow you can go round to Lady Harrison's house.'

The indifference in his tone would have hurt Vanessa bitterly once, but now she knew him better, could read his voice. He was trying to hide whatever it was he felt for her. She did not know if he loved her as she loved him; she supposed not, for how could anyone deny the glorious surge of feeling that was love? But he was not indifferent, and wanted to pretend that he was!

She had felt happy all day, and even knowing that they must soon part could not altogether dispel her happiness. So he was a libertine and a fortune hunter, who would deny even affection for her because he thought her a pauper. It simply made no difference. She loved him still and could not unlove him just because he was unworthy!

When it was dark, they set off. She held the dun mare back, cradling Curly in her cloak, wondering whether Jerome was taking the opportunity to press his suit with Mathilda.

He was, but half-heartedly. Automatically, almost, as though he could no more stop himself flirting with an heiress than fly. But his thoughts were with the small, copper-topped figure on the mare. A darling, that's what she was! She had found time and the opportunity to whisper to him that Mathilda was not indifferent; that she truly was interested in him as a suitor, and that he should pop the question towards the end of the Season. His heart should have lifted; it had not. His gambling instinct seemed to have failed him since he'd met Vanessa. He glanced down at Mathilda's golden head, nodding sleepily against his shoulder, and felt not a pang of desire nor of interest, even.

Then he shook himself. Nevertheless, if the opportunity arose, he must marry her!

It was a long ride, but they reached Hanover Square at last. Mathilda slipped from his horse, smiled up at him, and then walked as wearily as if she had really covered miles on foot, to the front door. It opened, bright light streaming out onto the flagway. Mathilda spoke, was helped indoors, the door closed.

The two horsemen turned towards each other and grinned.

'Right. Part one of the plan completed. Now you'd best come back to my lodgings and change into your girl's clothing.'

She nodded. 'Very well. I suppose it's too late to go round to my Godmama's house tonight? I dread the thought of being alone in a hotel.'

'Well, it is late, but perhaps it might be possible. You'll have to tell her you caught the last stage and then had to walk from the inn. Come along.'

They rode through the street to his lodging a short distance away and he opened the door for her, thrust her into a cold and comfortless room with instructions to light the fire from the candle on the hall stand, and then took the horses round to the livery stable.

She felt very alone, in that strange house. She crossed the living room, the candle gripped tight in her fingers, and bent to light the fire. The wood was damp, but at last it flickered into life and almost at once, Jerome returned.

'You've lit it? Good. I had intended to give you a meal but my landlady seems to have gone on the gad and there's very little food in. Slip into the bedroom and change, there's a good girl. Don't worry, I won't . . .'

'I know you won't,' she said. 'Very well.'

He was prepared for a lengthy wait but she was no more than ten minutes and emerged with her

168

hair brushed into a cloud of curls, a green silk ribbon tying them back from her face, and the green silk gown he had seen her in before. She looked deathly tired and, for the first time that day, sad.

His heart smote him. What a dance he'd led her!

'You look worn out. Do you want to sit down for a bit before we tackle Lady Harrison?'

She conjured up a pale smile, shaking her head. 'No. Let's go, Jerome, before . . .'

He put her cloak round her shoulders and took her arm.

'Good lass! It isn't far, or I'd order a hansom. What will you say to your Godmama about your luggage — or the lack of it?'

'I shouldn't need to say anything, she'll know I've run away I daresay.'

They traversed the short distance in silence, and stood for a moment before the house.

'They go to bed early,' Vanessa said, a little dismayed by the quiet darkness. 'But then they've small children I believe.'

But Jerome had strode up to the front door and was examining it closely. He made no attempt to knock or ring, but turned on his heel and joined her once more on the flagway.

'Here's a thing! What do we do now?'

'Why? What's happened?'

'The Harrisons are out of town. They must have had word that you were not to come after all, and the knocker is tied up.'

169

CHAPTER
EIGHT

It was too much. Vanessa just stared at him blankly, like a whipped dog. She could think of nothing to say, nothing to do, except sit down on the flagway and howl, as Curly would probably have done.

Curly, who had trotted along beside them, tugged impatiently on the length of rope round his shoulders; Vanessa had refused to tie it round his neck again, she had seen how nearly he had been strangled when he jumped off the coach.

The long silence was broken at last by Jerome. 'Well, shall it be a hotel or will you return to my lodgings and sleep there with just Curly for company? I can go to my Club.'

She felt a tiny smile curl the corners of her mouth. The relief of not having to face a hotel at this time of night, with no luggage, no sort of reasonable explanation, and a small dog of doubtful origins!

'Could I? Oh, Jerome could I possibly stay at your lodgings?'

He took her elbow and began to steer her back along the street.

'Of course you could, if you really don't mind the discomfort attendant upon being alone. And Vanessa, my dear, I'm afraid it will be breeches again for a bit. My landlady, you see, knows that I frequently have friends to stay with me — cousins and the like — but she would not countenance a young woman spending the night under her roof, even if I were a million miles away.'

'I don't mind,' Vanessa said eagerly. 'Anything not to have to face a hotel tonight!'

Fortunately for both of them, Jerome's landlady had still not returned when they got back, so he locked his door, lit the candles, and made up the smouldering fire.

'Now what can we eat?'

'There's a lot of bottles here,' Vanessa said, prying into a cupboard. 'And some sort of sponge fingers, though they're awfully stale. And a bowl of nuts. And . . .'

'I keep my drink in here, for entertaining my friends,' Jerome said shortly. 'Here, hold on, I'll go and forage.'

He disappeared through the door but returned empty-handed.

'No use, you nip into the bedroom, Vanessa, and change back into breeches, just in case anyone sees you. I'm going out again. There are various places where I can procure us a meal.'

'Oh, it doesn't matter,' Vanessa said, eager to be as little trouble as possible. 'I'm not hungry . . . well, not terribly hungry.'

He was shrugging on his surtout and said briefly, 'Yes you are, or if you aren't, I am! I shan't be long! Pour yourself some wine or something and take a biscuit or two.'

He raised a hand and was gone, leaving Vanessa to wander forlornly back into the bedroom, change yet again, and then return to the living room.

She sat down in a very comfortable winged armchair and gazed at the fire. How bright it was! And beautifully warming, after the time she had spent in the cold air today. She patted her knees and Curly jumped up and whined at her. Poor little chap, he must be hungry too! She wondered if he would like a sponge finger. Or perhaps a biscuit; she didn't think he would fancy nuts.

She lifted him off her knee, put him in the armchair where her body had warmed the cushions, and went to the cupboard. She got out the sponge fingers, crumbled them (with some difficulty) into a large glass dish, and then looked around for something to soften them with. Of course, the wine, or whatever it was in the bottles.

It was the work of the moment to find a bottle which had been uncorked and loosely corked up again. She drew the cork and sniffed cautiously. Whew! Whatever it was, it certainly made one's eyes water! She poured it over the sponge fingers, patted it into mush with a long metal spoon which Jerome probably used for stirring hot punch, and presented it to Curly.

He was ravenous, poor little dog, she thought compassionately as he sniffed, took a doubtful lick and then wolfed the lot, chasing the last alcoholic crumb round the plate and snuffling it into his eager maw.

She made a little more of the same concoction and put it before him. He ate it with equal speed, his tongue swirled regretfully round the empty dish, and then he curled up before the fire, replete. Presently, his snores began to rumble round the room.

Vanessa glanced at the clock on the mantel; it seemed a long time since Jerome had left her, but the clock had stopped. She returned to her chair, then wondered if she might help herself to some wine. She looked at the sleeping dog. To sleep like that — a complete abandonment! Hastily, she sat down in the chair and curled her legs up under her. It would never do if she had a drop too much to drink — and certainly Curly's snores seemed to indicate that he was more soundly asleep than usual.

She blinked at the flames. Soon, Jerome would be back with some food, and then she could go to bed at last.

Her chin dropped onto her chest. Presently,

her curly head rested against the wing of the chair.

Almost as soundly as her little dog, Vanessa slept.

'Hey there! Harcourt, old man!'

The rumbustuous shouts assailed Vanessa's ears and brought her eyes half open, even as she began to uncurl from the cushions.

'Who . . . what . . . ?'

'Hello-hello-hello! Who's this, then? Tony, old boy, there's a stowaway on that chair! And bless me, an ill-favoured hound asleep on the mat! Whatever is the world coming to?'

The speaker, a tall, pink faced gentleman wearing a white tie wig and a splendid velvet coat with silver braiding, put a long stemmed glass to his eye and peered down at Vanessa.

'A red-haired stowaway, no less! Well, boy? What are you doing here? Haven't you a tongue in your head?'

'M . . . me?' stammered Vanessa. She knuckled her eyes vigorously, then opened them to their fullest extent. Sure enough, two totally strange men stood easily in the middle of the room, eyeing her with considerable interest.

'Yes, you me boy,' the second man said. He was shorter than his companion, with black, merry eyes, and he was wearing his own dark hair which had been dusted with a blue powder.

'I'm . . . I'm Jerome's cousin,' Vanessa said. 'And th . . . that's my dog!'

'Oho, and where's Jerome? It crossed my mind that we'd disturbed a thief at work when we first entered,' the man called Tony remarked. He grinned at Vanessa. 'However, I can see you're no thief; I'll wager you've been helping yourself to Jerome's brandy though, you young rascal! Now pour some for us!'

Vanessa got stiffly to her feet, swayed, then walked resolutely over to the cupboard whose swinging door had proclaimed her guilt. She chose two glasses and poured brandy into them with a generosity which made her uninvited guests blink.

'I say, steady,' the taller man said hastily. 'If you poured yourself a brandy like that it's a wonder you ain't bosky as an owl! Top it up with water for me.'

'W-water?' Vanessa looked wildly round the room, as though expecting to see a fountain spring out of the carpet. 'I . . . I don't know where the kitchen is!'

'You don't? How long have you been here, then?'

That was the man called Tony, eyeing her with interest.

Vanessa gulped and pulled herself together. She must wake up properly and remember she was a young man amongst men!

'About an hour, I believe. May I introduce myself? I'm Oliver Harcourt, and you are . . .'

'Oh, how de do?' That was the pink-faced one. 'I'm Matthew Colbert and this is Tony

Markham.' His ingenuous countenance took on a portentous frown. 'Oliver Harcourt? I didn't know . . .'

'You must have known Philip's reputation,' Tony Markham said, *sotto voce*. 'There were no *legal* heirs, I grant you . . .'

'Oh, he's love begot, is he?' Matthew said, his brow clearing. He stepped closer to Vanessa. 'Not much like the Harcourts though, is he? I mean, he's got red hair, and green eyes!'

'Like the mother, I daresay,' Tony said hastily. 'Look, I'll get some water!'

'Now if you'd said one of Jer's bye-blows, I could have put a name to the wench,' Matthew continued, oblivious of Vanessa's discomfiture. 'Never known such a chap for bedding with yaller-heads and red-heads! There was that fiery little piece on Egerton Street, and . . .' he stopped, looking hard at Vanessa. 'You're a bit too long in the tooth to be one of Jer's bye-blows though, I daresay? What are you? Twelve? Fourteen?'

'Er . . . Er . . .' stammered Vanessa. For the life of her she could not remember whether Jerome had ever mentioned how old Philip had been when he died! Drawing a bow at a venture, she concluded wildly, 'Not . . . not quite . . . er . . . fourteen.'

'Then you ain't of Jer's getting,' Matthew said, quite kindly. 'Or not unless he started before he was breached! He's not yet thirty is he, Tony?'

Tony, entering with a jug of water in one hand,

gestured to the brimming brandy glasses in Vanessa's wobbly grasp.

'Is he what? Put the glasses down on the table, lad, and then you'd best tip a tiny bit out of each so's I can get some water in!'

'Not too much water in mine,' Matthew said, watching the jug as it was tilted. 'Whoa, there, that's plenty, never drown good brandy!' He took his glass. 'Your health, young whatsisname!'

'Oh, er, thank you,' Vanessa said. She seized the third glass, into which both young men had tipped a little unwanted brandy, and sipped it. Quickly, before she could change her mind, she tilted the rest of the brandy down her throat, then smiled, through watering eyes, at her companions. 'Your h-health, gentlemen!'

To her horror, both young men then proceeded to make themselves comfortable, Matthew stretching out on the small sofa and Tony sitting in the wingchair opposite her own.

'Well, this is snug. How long's Jerome been gone, lad?'

That was Matthew, from his cushioned comfort.

'An hour or so, I think,' Vanessa said, frowning at the clock. 'I can't think why he's so long, for he only went out to fetch us something to eat.'

Tony raised his brows. 'Something to eat? Why on earth didn't he take you to the Club? Not saying it's the best dinner in London but it's good enough for a cousin. What has he gone to fetch? Pig's trotters and gravy?'

'Well, I don't . . . why should he bring pig's trotters?' Vanessa asked curiosity overcoming her.

'They don't serve them at the Club,' Tony said briefly. 'It's my belief, youngster, that Jer was gammoning you when he said he'd gone to fetch food. You know why he's come to Town, of course?'

'Well, I sort of know,' Vanessa said.

'Aye, so do we all! It's my belief that he's nipped off to make sure *everyone* knows he's turned respectable, if you know what I mean?'

Matthew, from the sofa, said: 'Why should it matter if everyone knows? He's on the trail of an heiress, ain't he?'

'Don't be crude, Matt. The point is that if Meggie Conquest or Becky Clarke or even the little dancer he was carrying on with approach him for a bit of fun, he could be in queer street with the heiress. Best be above board, that's my motto. I'll lay Jer's gone the rounds, to warn the ladies off!'

Vanessa was about to air her views when a voice from the doorway said softly, 'Keeping an eye on my business as usual, Tony? I'll thank you not to make it public!'

Jerome lounged into the room without a glance at Vanessa, and poured himself a brandy.

Vanessa felt the colour flood her face in a humiliating tide. She poked her noble hound with one foot.

'Curly! Come along, old fellow, I'll take you

for a walk and then we must retire before we fall asleep on our feet.'

Despite her words and her nudge, Curly continued to snore. Jerome walked over and squatted near the animal, tickling his whiskers with one long forefinger.

'What have you done to this dog, coz? He's dead to the world!'

'Oh, dear,' faltered Vanessa. 'I thought I gave him sponge fingers soaked in wine, coz, but I very much fear that it was brandy? Can he . . . can he be *inebriated?*'

There was a shout of laughter from the three young men.

'Inebriated? Drunk as a wheelbarrow,' shouted Tony. 'I never thought I'd see a dog drunk on Jer's brandy!'

Jerome picked the luckless hound up and dangled him in the air. Curly, undisturbed by such cavalier treatment, slumbered on.

'Best take him out, coz,' Jerome advised. 'He'll wake, I daresay, when he feels the fresh air. If he doesn't, I should prefer that he sleeps it off outside rather than in my lodgings. If he's ill during the night he can be ill on the flagway and not on my carpets!'

He dumped the dog unceremoniously in Vanessa's arms and turned to address his companions.

Vanessa trailed outside with Curly snugly clasped in her arms, waited for a moment on the flagway, and then stood Curly down on the ground. Or rather, endeavoured so to do. But the poor creature's legs would not take his weight. They simply buckled under him and he descended into a heap on the ground, his eyes still shut, small snores still issuing from his quivering nose.

After three or four attempts she snatched Curly up from the flagway and marched back into the house. The three men were laughing over something, all with a drink in their possession, but Vanessa was tired, cross, and sick of being ordered about.

'I can't make him wake up,' she said angrily, cutting across whatever it was that Matthew was saying. 'I'm going to bed!'

She went to march past Jerome and was stopped short in her tracks by a stinging blow across the face which brought tears to her eyes, and made her gasp and cringe back, appalled.

'Don't talk to me like that, youngster,' Jerome said. His voice sounded quite casual. 'I know you're tired out, but you're only a lad! Curl up on the coach there whilst we finish our brandy!'

'But . . . but I want to go to *bed*,' Vanessa said, her voice breaking on a sob. 'C-can't I g-go to b-bed now? I'm so tired!'

She was facing Jerome and saw a flicker of feeling in his dark eyes — read the warning there, too. Of course, a young lad would never behave like that to the man under whose roof he was staying, particularly an uncle! She gasped, giving an almost imperceptible nod.

'I'm sorry, Jerome, I forgot my manners. May I get the pallet out in your chamber, and lie down until your friends have left? Then I'll bring it through here.'

With easy comradeship he put his arm round her shoulder, ruffling her curls.

'You're not a bad lad! Yes, I daresay Matt and Tony will excuse you. You've had a long day of it — and so have I, fellows, so if you'll drink up . . .'

As she went through the bedroom door and closed it softly behind her, Vanessa heard Matthew saying, '. . . get something to eat! I told him you'd best dine at the Club, but . . .'

But she was past caring. All she wanted was to sleep.

Yet oddly enough, now that she was alone in the dim light of the one candle, with the men's voices muted by the heavy door, she no longer felt so exhausted. She prowled about, finding a shirt of Jerome's which she decided to sleep in so that she could strip all her clothes off for the first time for what seemed like months. Then she poured cold water into the basin and washed her face and hands. Presently, she heard voices raised in farewell, and knew herself to be alone. She had stripped and put on Jerome's shirt, and was actually standing in the bowl of water, washing her feet, when there was a tap at the door and it opened.

'Hey!' she exclaimed, startled.

Jerome's face broke into a broad grin.

'Paddling, Oliver? You must have drunk as

181

much brandy as that cur of yours! I just thought I'd best warn you that I shan't be sleeping at the Club after all.'

She stood on one foot in the bowl, feeling foolish and extremely vulnerable. To give her self-confidence, she said haughtily: 'Why not? I certainly don't intend to share your bed again!'

His smile faded. 'Since Matt and Tony have just gone off to the Club, it would look mighty strange if I went off there to sleep, leaving a four-teen-year-old stripling and a drunken dog to fend for themselves in my lodgings. Otherwise, my dear, I would keep my word and give you a wide berth.'

That stung. She stepped right out of the water and said sharply, 'Why do you say that? Or was it true what Matt and Tony said? That you didn't go out to get us some supper at all, but to sever your connections with the 'fiery little piece' you had in keeping, to say nothing of Meg, and . . . and . . .'

She faltered to a stop, awed by the look on his face.

'Just what do you mean by that?'

He hurled the words at her, his face whitening.

'Why, that . . . that you've visited your women, so want none of me,' she spat at him, throwing caution to the winds. 'Go on then, sniff round every stupid red-head and blonde in town! See if I care! But if you do that, then I hold my tongue with Mat . . .'

He was across the room in a stride, shaking her

until her teeth rattled in her head.

'So you think I want none of you? By God, but you shall learn different!' He eyed her insultingly, his glance going up and down the shirt as though it were made of glass. 'I must say, you've a body to tempt a saint! And I, madam, am no saint, as you seem determined to prove!' He seemed to recollect himself suddenly, letting go of her arms, putting his hand up to his head. 'My God, but you're an infuriating piece! If you're found one day with your neck wrung I shan't blame the murderer a bit.'

She was as horrified by the encounter as he now seemed to be. She said, her voice breaking, 'Jerome, I must be mad, I can't think what made me say such a stupid, unforgivable thing. I didn't think I had drunk much of that brandy, but I must have a very weak head. Please forgive me!'

For the first time, she thought he looked truly careworn.

'The sooner we part the better it will be for both of us, for if ever two people were born to bring out the worst in each other, it's us! Good-night, my child.'

She stood forlornly on the pink carpet, with her wet feet darkening it, whilst he strode from the room and shut the door firmly behind him without looking back.

In the guest-bedroom in the Remington's Hanover Square House, Mathilda woke, unable for a moment to think where she was. When, glancing around, she recognised the delightful room where her Godmama had brought her the night before, her first thought was one of relief that, at last, she had arrived. Her Season was about to begin.

Her second thought, much more creditably, was for her friend. Yesterday, she thought, had been a nightmare from the first moment of waking until Jerome had let her down from his horse and had watched her entry into his uncle's house. But for Vanessa, what had followed? She had been tempted, yesterday, to tell Jerome that he must restore Vanessa to her Aunt Nessie and to Bascombe Hall. After all, this Godmama had never seen fit to invite her Goddaughter to visit her before, had never shown the slightest interest in the girl. How could they know that Vanessa would be happy there? Would be accepted, even?

Now, she lay in her comfortable bed, with the sunlight slanting through the slats of the shutters, and wondered whether Vanessa had been kindly received. Had Lady Harrison welcomed her with open arms or with cold suspicion? After all, Jerome's plan for his Mama to introduce Vanessa and Lady Harrison had gone sadly awry.

She was telling herself that she must go round to George Street that very day and enquire after Vanessa, when there was a tapping at her door and it opened, to show her newly squired maid, Ruth, standing in the doorway balancing a tray in one hand and trying to push the door wide with the other.

'Morning, Miss,' she said cheerfully as she succeeded in entering the room. 'It's a lovely day Miss, and Milady's sent you up her favourite saffron buns to your breakfast.'

'They look lovely,' Mathilda said, gratefully sniffing the aroma of hot chocolate and freshly baked buns. 'Are you to help me to dress, Ruth?'

'Yes, Miss. And Milady says to come down as soon as may be, if you please, because she's got a very special surprise for you.'

'How lovely!' Mathilda exclaimed. It did cross her mind that most of the surprises she had received lately had been far from lovely, but she did not let this sour thought linger. She was in her own element now, in a rich man's well-ordered mansion with every day planned, every amusement carefully thought out. Oh, it had been fun to be free for a few days, but it was very nice to return to normality, after all!

'And there are French rusks, Miss, with black-currant jam,' the maid went on, plainly bent on impressing the young lady. 'And Milady's ordered the carriage, so's she can take you round the shops, to buy some bits of things. She said until your own luggage arrived you'd need extras.'

'I adore shopping,' Mathilda announced. She finished the last saffron bun and jumped out of bed. 'Help me into the rose-coloured walking

185

dress, Ruth, if you please, with the stout little kid boots, and the striped toilinette petticoat.'

Unlike her friend, Mathilda was not a speedy dresser; it was the best part of an hour later that, hair brushed into fat yellow ringlets, a ribbon tied at a coquettish angle, the rose walking dress donned, and the kid boots buttoned, she set out down the stairs.

At the foot of them she hesitated. Which way should she turn for the morning room, where she would find her hostess? A discreet cough brought her attention to a handsome footman, who said, 'This way, Miss,' and flung open a door.

She saw her hostess, standing facing the door and smiling, saying: 'Here she is! I trust, dearest, that you're refreshed after your sleep? I've told your little friend all about your dreadful experience yesterday and she was so relieved that you managed to escape and find your way safe to us! But you can see for yourself who else is to stay with me! She arrived in a coach from the North West, first thing this morning, to stay with Lady Harrison, but poor Millie's children have the measles, and Millie's gone rushing off to Surrey, never dreaming that her godchild was going to accept her invitation! So, naturally, when Jerome saw the child weeping in the street and heard her story, he brought her here.'

Vanessa, standing forlornly beside her hostess in her old green gown, now much crushed and crumpled, said diffidently, 'Hello, dear Matty! I

186

am sorry to invade your very first day in London with my presence, but I'm in a bit of a scrape!'

Mathilda took a deep, steadying breath.

'Vanessa, my darling, how *wonderful* to see you! And what a dreadful story! Is your dear little dog with you?'

Vanessa looked hunted, for she had seen the martial gleam in her friend's eyes.

'Why . . . why yes, but he won't trouble you, truly,' she stammered. 'He's gone off to the kitchens very happily with John, the second footman! I wish I could send him back to my Aunt, but he'd pine, I'm afraid, and that I could never bear.'

Lady Remington, a garrulous but good-natured woman, looked from one face to the other. Her nephew had been so certain that Miss Randolph would welcome the younger girl, but it seemed to her that Mathilda Randolph was far from pleased by her friend's sudden appearance. Could it be that there was something between them, some girlish feud over a young man, perhaps?

Fortunately, Mathilda had a warm heart, and she could not but feel sorry for Vanessa's plight. After all, she reasoned, though she was a considerable heiress herself, she had not half the money and property which would one day come to her friend. Yet far from envying her in such things, she could only feel sorry for the younger girl. No father or mother to love her, only a foolish old aunt who cared first and foremost for her own offspring. No good, kind Godparents to fire her off for her first Season, but a guardian who envied Vanessa her property and plotted to make it his son's. All she had got to love, in effect, was that horrid little dog!

She glided across the carpet and put her arms caressingly round Vanessa's slim shoulders.

'Poor Van, I shouldn't tease you about Curly! I do love dogs, but he's fond of you and no one else, that's the truth of the matter! Now, what exciting things shall we do today?'

'Oh, Matty, you are a darling,' Vanessa exclaimed, returning the embrace with fervour. 'Mr Harcourt has been so kind, as well, he's gone rushing down to Surrey to my Godmama's house, to ask her whether she might come back so that I can go to some dances and parties.'

The kindly Lady Remington, much relieved that the girls had obviously forgotten any differences, said heartily: 'No need for that, my dear; as I said, Millie's an old friend of mine and anyway, you'll be company for Mathilda! You're welcome to stay with us until she returns to Town or until the Season's over, come to that.'

'And we are to go shopping, so we'll buy you some really nice clothes,' Mathilda said, eager to make up for her earlier coldness. 'You'll want a great many things, and of course most of the clothes will have to be made, so the sooner we go out, the better.'

Despite herself, Vanessa's eyes began to sparkle. Pretty clothes were irresistible!

'That would be nice, but . . .'

'If you're worried about your allowance, don't,' Mathilda said bracingly. 'I know your guardian gives you as little as he dare, but when my Papa tells him he's been franking you, he will pay up with the appearance of complacency. Why, the Randolphs and the Talbots have been neighbours for ever!'

Presently, the two girls went out to get ready for their shopping expedition, leaving Lady Remington in a very thoughtful frame of mind. Jerome had gone to some pains to explain that Miss Norris, though a girl of gentle birth from one of the best families, was nevertheless in straitened circumstances. No whisper of the name 'Talbot' had passed his lips and knowing her nephew as she did, Lady Remington was very sure that had he known there was a connection, Jerome would have mentioned it.

For Frederick Talbot was known to be a rich though miserly fellow, with a mean, ferret-faced son who had expectations of marrying into a great deal of money. There had been a mention of the Bascombe Estates falling to young Talbot through some boy and girl romance.

Lady Remington put her head in her hands and tried to remember. It had been Millie Harrison who first mentioned the matter to her, in connection with a girl . . . she did her best to remember the very words Millie had used, but they escaped her now.

Presently, she gave up, but that did not mean

189

to say she had forgotten. There was some mystery about the little Norris girl; she was very sure that Mathilda had not meant to let the name Talbot slip out, and equally sure that neither girl had noticed the fact. She made her way up to her room to fetch her gloves and hat, and to don her light cloak, for it was a beautiful day. She guessed that, as soon as his errand in Surrey was accomplished, Jerome would be a constant visitor to Hanover Square. His intention, she knew, was to fix the heiress's interest if such a thing was possible. She must find out what, if anything, her nephew knew about the quiet little girl who called herself Vanessa Norris, and who had some connection with the Talbot family!

CHAPTER
NINE

It could be fairly said that the two days which followed were the happiest Vanessa could remember for a long, long time. She was a petted and honoured guest, yet no one could be accused of being friendly with her because she was heiress to the Bascombe estate, for no one knew she was anything other than Miss Vanessa Norris! Mathilda knew, of course, but Matty had always known and to be fair to her, she was so rich herself that to toadeat others would never have occurred to her.

On the evening of the second day, Jerome was to dine with them, to give Vanessa the messages which her Godmother had sent.

Though she could not have said why, Vanessa took especial pains with her appearance. She powdered her hair lightly, she borrowed an emerald necklace from her hostess which must have been worth thousands, she appeared for the first time in a ravishing evening dress of pale orange tulle, cut low over her bosom, and she wore a small, heartshaped patch near her mouth.

She walked into the Crimson saloon, and heard a gratifying intake of breath from Jerome. She smiled at him; wickedly, teasingly. She moved across to him, holding out her hand, saying aloud, 'You were so good to visit Lady Harrison for me!' and then, beneath her breath: 'Is this an improvement on your shirt, dear Jerome?'

For an instant his eyes devoured her, hotly caressing her bare shoulders, the clean line of her neck, her sparkling face. Then he murmured, 'I preferred you in the shirt,' and before she could do other than blush most delightfully he added, aloud, 'Lady Harrison sends you her dearest love, and promises to return to George Street in seven or eight days at the latest.'

'That is good of her. Did she . . . did she say anything when she got my note?'

But she knew the answer. If her Godmama had given her secret away, had told Jerome that she was Vanessa Bascombe, she would have known it from the first words he spoke. She heaved a sigh. Of course, she had no desire to be loved for her money and property, but oh, what bliss it would be to be loved by Jerome! She thought of his arms round her, his mouth crushing hers, and the room swam before her eyes. But he knew nothing of her feelings, merely saying politely, 'She laughed, so I collect you told her some of the more repeatable of your adventures! She is a very sensible and delightful person, my child, and you'll soon grow fond of one another I'm sure.'

'Good! Then I shall look forward . . .'

She was interrupted. The butler stepped forward and murmured something in Lady Remington's ear. Lady Remington smiled, spoke a few words, and then held up her hand to her guests, who had been about to depart to the dining room.

'Wait a moment, if you please. Craythorpe has gone to lay another place at table, for we have another guest! Jerome, my dear, your Mama has arrived, after a most wearisome journey. Vanessa, Mathilda, make your curtsies to Mrs Demetria Harcourt!'

Demetria had planned this moment. She had reached London earlier that afternoon to find not a whisper in the Beau Monde about her son and the heiress. Not one person looked sideways at her, asked her veiled questions, tutted over her son's behaviour whilst secretly envying it!

She had discovered speedily enough that Jerome had arrived in London with a young person, and a few questions at the livery stable which her son frequented had made her positive that Jerome had indeed abducted the heiress, had actually brought her back to his own lodgings after his night of love, had then proceeded to take her to the Remington's house — and had done nothing further!

193

She had known, for a moment, quite murderous rage. To behave in so lily-livered a fashion made her doubt that he was her own flesh and blood! The Harcourts took what they wanted, they did not allow themselves to be deflected from their course by the pleas of a young girl, be she never so pretty!

Then, in a moment, she had seen what she must do. She would go to the house at a time when all were assembled together, so that there could be no covering up, and she would Tell All! Then there could be no turning back. Jerome would marry the heiress, plain or pretty, winsome or loathsome, and her own troubles would be over.

And now, she faced them. Her eyes skimmed quickly over the assembled company. Her brother, her silly sister-in-law, her son, white-faced. He was flanked by two girls, both, to her surprise, pretty. The blonde young thing who had been so impudent to her at that little inn, and another. Demetria's eyes widened. An adorable child, just the sort of girl a man would run mad for! The rest of the company were useful merely as witnesses; a peer and his wife, a distant cousin, a young man friend of Jerome's, brought in to make up the numbers.

'So, my son! I find you and your paramour here, in my own brother's house!'

Until she spoke there had been small movements, the two girls curtsying, the men manoeuvring to take their partners for dinner. Now, silence. No one spoke but stood as if stunned.

Demetria turned to the company.

'My son, made reckless by love, stole this young thing away, took her to a place that only he knows of, and seduced her! Yes, seduced her, Sir Thomas! I know not what wiles she used to keep this thing a secret, but I knew that I must Speak Out. I must insist that my son marry the girl — nay, the child — he has so shamefully dishonoured. I beg you to remember, friends, that anything he did, he did in the name of love!'

She surged forward, seizing the girl's hands, then her son's hard, brown fingers. She pressed the two hands together, hoping devoutly that the girl was not going to faint. She looked quite white, her eyes black with horror.

'Do you deny it, my son? Do you deny — *dare* you deny — that you stole this innocent away, and dishonoured her?'

She looked mournfully at Jerome, prepared for red-hot rages, for white-hot temper, even for a shamefaced compliance in her careful scheme. But instead, he was laughing, laughing so hard that he could scarcely answer her. She stepped back, her temper beginning to rise.

'You dare to *laugh?* Do you dare to deny that you abducted this innocent girl?'

He was shaking his head, the laughter ebbing, his hand grasping the girl's hand tightly.

'No, my dear Mama, I certainly do not deny it! Oh, my God, this is rich! Certainly I abducted this innocent girl. Oh, Demetria, when you know what you've done!'

'Done? What do you mean, you fool?'

He was beginning to laugh again, but there was a desperation in his laughter which frightened her so that she took a step backwards, her hand going to her throat.

'It's the wrong girl, dear Mama! This is Miss Norris, just a nice, ordinary little girl, and this young lady is Miss Mathilda Randolph, the heiress! And with your own silver tongue, Mama, you've made quite certain that I marry the penniless Miss Norris to save her reputation from your accusations, whilst the heiress goes her own way, untroubled by either of us!'

Mathilda was looking from one face to the other, baffled, uneasy, her hands half held out, as if to beg for an explanation. Vanessa stood as if turned to stone whilst her reputation crumbled around her, she saw herself mocked as a loose woman, and the laughter of the only man she would ever love rang in her ears.

Demetria gasped, clawed the air, turned a dark puce, and fell on the floor. She moaned, writhed, spittle bubbling from her dark lips. A horrible, terrifying sight.

The assembled company rushed forward, except Jerome and Vanessa, still standing with her hand in his, but a hand cold as ice.

'Don't worry over her,' Jerome said scornfully. 'She's done it before and she'll do it again. The two things she detests most in the world are being crossed, and being made a fool of; both those things have just happened to her, and so she's throwing a fit to take everyone's attention away from her stupidity and low cunning.'

'Don't speak of your mother like that,' Sir Thomas said sharply. 'Do something, man! Is there no restorative . . . ?'

'Yes, there's a phial in her pocket.' Jerome released Vanessa's little, cold fingers and bent over his mother's form, his mouth set with distaste. 'God, she makes me sick!' He found the phial, broke the top off, poured the liquid between her livid lips. He said, over his shoulder, 'I meant it, brat! Marry you I shall, and I daresay you'll live to regret it.'

He straightened as Demetria's body suddenly became quieter. Her lids drooped and then as abruptly as she had cast herself to the floor her limbs relaxed and she appeared to sleep.

'She's in a sort of coma,' Jerome said briefly. He rose to his feet, dusting his hands together. 'Sir Thomas, she's your sister, so you must have seen these fits before. Get the servants to take her to bed and see a maid stays with her. She'll be her usual self in the morning.'

Lady Remington, clutching her lord's arm, said faintly, 'I've never seen Demetria do that! It terrified me!'

'She had fits like that as a child,' Sir Thomas admitted. 'But I thought she'd got over them years since. It was always the same when she was small; let a child take her toy away, or someone else win a game, and she would throw a terrible tantrum. The doctor said it was just temper and too much self-love, but I thought she had finished with such displays.'

'She only did it once whilst my father lived,' Jerome said, with a mirthless grin. 'He took one look at her, I've been told, and then beat her until she scarcely could stand — nor sit neither, I dare swear. That cured her for years, but then she found her fits frightened my brother Philip and later, her lovers gave in rather than face . . .' he gestured to her inanimate form . . . 'that, and so it has gone on.' He glanced round. 'I do trust my prospective bride doesn't think there's madness in the family, after watching Demetria overact!'

Mathilda, who had been staring, fascinated, at Jerome, said in a small voice, 'I think Van's gone to be sick. She pressed her hands to her mouth and ran up the stairs.'

Jerome glanced up the stairs, then back to his mother. 'Uncle, do get someone to fetch her away. I don't intend to lay a finger on her, or I might follow my father's excellent example. As, indeed, I would to any woman of mine who behaved in so uncontrolled a fashion.' He slapped his forehead. 'Bless me, no use threatening the woman when she's not here. I'd best go up to her room and see that she's all right.'

'You can't . . .' Lady Remington began, then stopped, biting her lip.

'Can I not? My dear Aunt, since I am to marry the girl because I seduced her, took her to my lodgings for a night of love as my Mama rather theatrically put it, there can surely be no objection to my seeking her out now, to tell her to smile and wipe her tears? I can promise you I shan't throw her on the bed and . . .'

'Jerome, that's *enough*,' his uncle thundered. 'I don't know how much truth there was in your mother's devilish accusations, but I do know that poor little soul is in great distress. Leave her alone, sir. Maria?'

'Yes, dear?' his wife quavered, impressed to see her usually mild husband so irate.

'Go up to your guest — take Miss Mathilda with you, if she'll consent to go — and tell that child that we don't believe a word of it and that Jerome shall marry her, and we'll make all right. Tell her . . . confound it, woman, you must know what she most wants to hear!'

'Of my demise, I should think,' said the irrepressible Jerome.

'I said that was enough! Good God, that I should live to see a nephew of mine break the heart of an innocent maid, no matter what else you did, sir, and then . . .'

Jerome crossed to his uncle's side and laid a hand on his shoulder.

'I swear to you sir, on my life, that she's innocent still! I meant . . . confound it, I meant to seduce her, but . . .'

'I don't want to *know*,' cried his harassed relative. 'Not but what I'm relieved to hear it Jerome, for I never did think you as black as you were

199

painted. And now for the love of God ring for the servants to move your Mother before she drives me as insane as she appeared to be herself!'

For a short while, there was a bustle in the hall as the manservants brought a door off its hinges to carry the afflicted Demetria to her room. Jerome, glancing at her with loathing, muttered to his friend Sollars, who had been an extremely embarrassed bystander, 'She's round now, the wicked old devil, but shamming like anything. See her lids flicker?' He grinned at his friend's pink face. 'My, Sollars, but won't you have a story to tell round the Clubs tomorrow?'

'Upon my word, Harcourt, not a word . . . wouldn't dream . . . been a friend of yours too long . . .' muttered the young man, putting a finger into his collar, which suddenly seemed too tight.

'I hope you remember that,' Jerome said pleasantly. 'Otherwise, my dear old fellow, you're going to find yourself with a bullet through the belly! And that goes for anyone who says a word against Miss Norris. As for my dear Mama and her fancy fits, you can spread that bit of nonsense throughout the land for all I care!'

'Fond of her then, Jer?' his friend remarked boldly, jerking his chin towards the stairs.

'Devilish fond. No one I'd rather marry, if I had to marry anyone,' Jerome said rather gloomily. 'I just hate the thought that I've been . . . well, caught. Tricked, trapped, pushed into it.'

'Not true, though,' Sollars pointed out diffidently. 'If you *didn't* . . . hrrmph . . . then there's no earthly reason why you should marry her.'

'Perhaps not. Aha, here comes my Aunt. Let's hear how my poor little one is.'

It occurred to Sollars, not a particularly percipient young man, that his friend's hard face softened a great deal when he spoke of the girl, and that now his eyes were fixed on his aunt with painful, almost shy enquiry in their depths.

'Well, Aunt Maria? Does she want me? Is she very distressed?'

'No, she's not very distressed. Or perhaps she is, but she wouldn't admit it. She says she won't marry you, you shan't be made to marry anyone, and she'll explain it all in the morning.'

'But . . . but I must see her *now*,' Jerome said, almost at a loss for words. 'Damn it, Aunt Maria, I said things just now which I would bite my tongue out if she took literally! She's not to blame for any of it! I swear . . .'

'Leave it, Jerome. The girl needs time to think. In the morning . . .'

'Damn the morning, I say,' roared Jerome, cutting across his uncle's sage advice. 'I must and will see her now!'

He pushed past his uncle and aunt, took the stairs two at a time, and burst into the smaller of the two guest rooms on the top landing which he guessed would be Vanessa's.

There was nothing there. No one. He glanced

round wildly, then dashed out of the door.

Mathilda was emerging into the corridor from another room.

'Is she in there? I must talk to her.'

Mathilda looked bewildered.

'There's no one in there. She was in her room, with the door locked. She must be in there still, but not answering.'

He grabbed her arm, ignoring her cry of pain, and dragged her to the next doorway.

'Look, you stupid, empty-headed female! Is she there?'

'Let go of my arm, Jerome Harcourt, *I'm* not in love with you!' Mathilda said forcibly. 'Of course she's not there, she must have gone downstairs.'

'How? We were all in the hall, and . . . the back stairs!'

He rushed for them, descended three at a time, arriving in the kitchen out of breath and looking quite wild enough, one of the kitchenmaids said later, to turn the milk sour.

'Has Miss Norris gone through here?'

'Oh yes, sir,' a small maid ventured. 'Ten, fifteen minutes ago, with her little dog under her arm. Taking him into the stableyard for an airing she said she was.'

Jerome, with a curse, dashed out into the stableyard. It was deserted. He searched the stables, the haylofts, the outbuildings. He roamed the streets, calling for Vanessa, calling Curly, employing every ragged urchin in sight to search

202

for a lady in a pale orange dress, with her hair powdered.

No one had seen her. She appeared to have vanished off the face of the earth.

If he had looked a little more carefully he might have discovered why Terror was so indifferent to his mangerful of hay. Because it was not hay, it was an orange tulle gown and a toilinette petticoat. Then he might have investigated a little further, and made enquiries for a shabby little servant girl in a hooded cloak and a crushed green gown with a little dog on a length of rope.

But by the time the clothes were found hidden in the hay, Vanessa was miles beyond Jerome's reach.

In fact, she very nearly got into trouble within a mile of Hanover Square. Wandering along with Curly prancing beside her, desperately wondering where to go and what to do until morning, she was approached by a tall, skinny person with dark and sombre clothing and the look of extreme respectability common, had she known it, amongst those who seek to deceive the innocent.

'My dear child, you should not be wandering the streets at this time of night! Do not fear me, for I am a man of God, and will help you, if I can. I can recommend an excellent lodging house, where . . .'

So tired and unhappy was she that Vanessa

would have leapt at the offer but Curly, knowing nothing of refined accents or respectable clothing, recognised a fellow rogue at once and pulled back against his mistress's skirt, curling his lip and uttering a horrifying snarl.

'The woman who runs this house might easily be woken, and persuaded to take you in; she's a good, Christian soul, and her mission in life is to help those less fortunate than herself.' He took a step towards her, his smile proving, on closer acquaintance, to belong to an elderly gentleman of quite forty-five, which dispelled any doubts Vanessa might have harboured. A man so elderly must be respectable! 'Let me take your arm, my dear!'

At this point Curly endeavoured to take the gentleman's ankle and succeeded in obtaining a piece of his respectable breeches.

The dark-coated gentleman leapt back with a word which was strange to Vanessa, and begged her to keep her dog under control.

'I don't think he likes you,' Vanessa said doubtfully. She was beginning to wonder whether she much liked the gentleman herself.

The gentleman, recovering, laughed genially.

'Tis often the way with little dogs. Clerics are either a race they love or can't abide. I fear your little dog, ma'am, has a dislike for the Church.'

'Oh, are you a clergyman?' Vanessa said, vastly relieved. 'Well then, I should be most grateful for your assistance. Curly, behave!'

But Curly was quite intelligent enough to

know when to obey commands and when to disobey. He drew back against his mistress's skirt once more and began to bark, snarling whenever he ran out of breath. And as soon as the dark-coated gentleman came nearer, in order to shout something to Vanessa, he launched a vicious attack.

There followed the sort of scene the dark-coated gentleman most wished to avoid. Shouts, barks, screams — regrettably, his own — and general pandemonium, whist the little dog tore at his clothing, attacked his skinny calves until the blood ran, and finally chased him up the street.

Two chairmen, carrying a client home from a party, stopped, stood their chair down, and went over to the small, cloaked figure staring mournfully up the road.

'What 'appened, Miss? Did 'e try to molest you?'

The small person turned round eyes up to his.

'I'm not sure that the boot wasn't on the other foot. He was a clergyman, offering me a respectable bed in a respectable house for the night, and my dog attacked him! I feel so mortified!'

'A clergyman? 'im? Naw, that was Smooth-tongued Charlie, and you did oughter *fank* your little dog! That weren't no 'spectable 'ouse 'e recommended, that were . . .'

Someone leaned out of the chair, someone with a pair of merry black eyes and a drawling voice. He began to speak when suddenly, he found a small, vaguely familiar face within inches of his own, his hands were clasped in a desperate clasp, and a voice he had heard somewhere before rang in his ears.

'Tony! Oh, thank God, it's Tony! Would you help me, sir? I am quite desperate, for that wicked man was not a clergyman at all — and indeed I must have known it when he swore so dreadfully rudely at poor Curly! I've run away from . . .'

Light suddenly dawned. Tony's mouth dropped open, then was firmly controlled.

'By God, it's Jerome's little cousin! Philip's bye-blow! What in heaven's name. . . .'

'Oh sir, do you have a home and a respectable Mama, who might take pity on me, just for one night? I am at my wits end!'

Tony climbed out of the sedan chair, paid some money over to the highly interested chairmen, and bade them, rather sharply, to take themselves off. As soon as they had done so he turned to Vanessa in time to see Curly return, tail wagging, and a piece of cloth dangling from his jaws.

'Look, you'd best come to my lodgings,' Tony said, indicating a nearby house. 'Don't worry about . . . well, to be frank, I ain't in the habit of dressing wenches up in breeches to deceive my friends and then seducin' them and turnin' them into the street!'

'Nor's Jerome!' Vanessa fired up at once. 'He *found* me in breeches, and — and merely let me stay at his lodgings for one night, until I could go to my Godmama's. I've run away from there!'

'Oh, I see,' Tony said, his brow clearing. He unlocked the door and ushered his companion into a pleasant, warm room with thick carpeting and a bright fire. 'And where are you running to, may I ask?'

'Well, I don't . . .' Vanessa glanced round the room, at the warmth and cosy normality of it. 'Home,' she said, her voice breaking a little. 'I wish I'd never run away, and now I want to go home to — to my home!'

She knew, at that moment, that she spoke no more than the truth. She had run away for adventure and goodness knows, she had found enough of that. She had fallen in love, laughed a lot, wept a lot, and now her heart was broken and all she wanted was to nurse it in secret, until it was whole again. Or if not whole, at least mended in the eyes of the world.

'Well, that's simple enough. Where do you live?'

'In the north. I know which coach to catch and where it leaves from, though not the times. And oh, Mr . . . oh Tony, if I promise on my word of honour that I'll repay you soon, could you possibly lend me some money to buy my ticket? I'll send the money to you, truly, and I'll never forget your kindness.'

'Yes, of course I'll lend you some money,' Tony said. 'But you'd best tell me why you fled from your Godmama's house. You didn't do anything foolish, I hope?'

'Oh no, truly! But Jerome's mother found out about my being in his lodgings and she came, and she shouted things about me which were not true, and said Jerome must marry me at once!'

He looked incredulously at her, his eyes travelling over the crumpled green gown, the stained kid boots.

'*Demetria* did? Are you sure?'

Vanessa laughed hollowly.

'I know what you're thinking, but you see she thought I was Miss Randolph. You know, the rich one. She saw me standing beside Jerome and Miss Randolph was on the side of him, and she sort of assumed . . .'

'Aye, I can just imagine.' He chuckled briefly. 'She thought to force a marriage between them, and overplayed her hand. The silly . . . but I daresay Jerome settled her hash!'

'I don't know. She fell on the ground and went all purple in the face, and the ladies and gentlemen who had been staring so hard at me began to stare at her instead. So I left.'

'Yes, and very wise, too. Now I don't intend to offer you my bed because I don't want to cause a scandal, but you may curl up on the sofa and welcome. I'll wake you at five — don't you go undressin', or anything like that! — and we'll find out when the first stage leaves for the north!'

CHAPTER
TEN

It was May, and London was blooming. In the parks and squares the flower beds were full of heavy-headed tulips, scarlet and gold, and with wallflowers, whose sweet, heady scent filled the air and brought thoughts of the country, and cottage gardens.

Mathilda was walking in the park. Wearing a new hat, new gloves, and carrying an elegant pink parasol which cast an enchantingly becoming shade over her golden hair and small, neat features, and with a gown on which had brought forth compliments from her considerable male acquaintance, she knew herself to be looking her best. And wasted, she thought bitterly, on present company.

Jerome walked beside her, made more handsome, if anything, by his haggard look, the pallor which lurked beneath his tan. He had managed to convince everyone that he had not seduced Miss Norris, that he had, in fact, behaved towards her in a gentlemanly fashion. Mathilda's Papa, visiting his daughter in Hanover Square, had been most impressed with Mr Harcourt; a quiet, sensible man, whose only interest in life seemed to be his dilapidated and encumbered estates. 'And my daughter, of course,' Mr Randolph had boomed proudly.

But Mathilda knew better. Jerome courted her, sought her company, simply because she could talk about Vanessa. She knew that Van was at home by now, and probably picking up the threads of her life satisfactorily, for she had received a note within two or three days of Vanessa's hurried departure, simply saying, *'I'm home. Don't tell. Van.'*

She had not told but sometimes, looking into Jereome's haunted eyes, she had been tempted.

And now, walking beside him through the park, she acknowledged a little sadly that he was present only in body. His mind was far away and though she could recall him easily enough he would answer her politely, with good-humour and his usual charm. But absentmindedly, she thought.

She saw the Miss Warrenders, and bowed, pinching Jerome's arm. He bowed too, and raised his hat, then continued to walk beside her, lost in a brown study.

'What a delightful day it is, Mr Harcourt. Yes indeed, Miss Randolph, though I daresay we'll have rain before nightfall. Do you think so, Mr Harcourt? I fear so, Miss Randolph.'

210

Mathilda conducted the conversation with herself solemnly, hoping to win a smile from Jerome, but all he said was, 'Yes indeed!'

Mathilda stopped dead in her tracks and stamped her foot. Her patience was at an end!

'Jerome, I want to be taken home, if you please, and then I want you to stop calling on me! This whole friendship is a farce! You form one of my court, you shoulder other suitors out of my life with your constant attention and invitations but you aren't in the least interested in me! I don't expect to fall wildly in love, that's servants' talk, but I *do* expect to marry someone who thinks me pretty to look at and interesting to talk to. All you think of is my money, which will bring your estate back into good heart, and my friend Vanessa, whom you shamefully mistreated!'

Jerome stopped walking too and faced her, animation in his expression for the first time, it seemed, for weeks.

'You're quite right, I don't want to form one of your wretched court, nor do I want to dance attendance upon you day and night, and pretend I find you fascinating. I don't find any woman fascinating! All I want out of life is Vanessa, and if I can't have her, then I damned well don't care if I go to the devil!'

He swung round, dragging her roughly with him.

'If you want Vanessa, why don't you try to find her?' Mathilda said waspishly, almost running to keep up with his long strides.

He turned on her, his eyes glowing with annoyance.

'Do you think I've not tried? I know she comes from the north west, probably not far from my own home. I know her name's Vanessa Norris and she has a little white dog called Curly. I've written to friends, I've journeyed to my home and questioned every person of quality I could find, I've written to every damned school in Harrogate because she went to school there, with you, but not a trace can I find. She might as well not exist!'

'And if you found her? What would you do then? I could help you, if . . .'

They were on the crowded flagway now and once more he stopped, seizing her hands in his, gripping them painfully tight.

'You know where she is? Mathilda, I'll . . . I'll . . .'

'Yes, I know where she is. But I *don't* know what your intentions are! For all I know she may have forgotten you already, and be happier by far left alone.'

The devils she had not seen in his eyes for so long were back, dancing.

'I'd soon cure her of that! Just let me get my arms round her . . .'

'Jerome, just listen to me! If I told you that she was the housekeeper's daughter on a big estate, and that she had been brought up by the lord of the manor as a companion for his own daughter, would you still want to find her?'

'Yes!'

She could not doubt him, the intensity of his feeling for her friend shone from his eyes, lighting his countenance.

'Well then . . . oh dear, I wonder if I ought!'

He pulled her into a shop doorway, as if to admire the display of kid gloves in the window, turned so that his broad back was between her and the crowds on the pavement, and put his hands lightly round her throat.

'My dear, if you don't tell me, you'll be dear, *dead* little Mathilda Randolph!'

She looked up into his face and did not doubt the threat for one moment.

'All right, I'll tell you. But . . . you'll do right by her, if she wants you to do so?'

'Of course I will, damn it,' he said impatiently. 'Tell me her direction!'

'Bascombe Hall, near Sedgeworth.'

He drew in a sharp breath.

'Bascombe Hall! But of course, a housekeeper's daughter . . . I'll get Terror saddled right away.'

He would have left her then and there but she clung to his arm, laughing at him.

'No, don't you *dare* abandon me in the street! Take me back to Hanover Square first!'

'Rhoda, my dear, where is your cousin?'

Rhoda, contentedly stitching at a new petti-coat, her mind upon her forthcoming nuptuals, glanced vaguely round the room.

'Isn't she in here? Oh, I suppose she's walked into the village, or perhaps she's down at the stables with that wretched dog. Why, Mama?'

Mrs Mordred's little, fat face wore a frown, and her forehead was creased with unaccustomed thought.

'I'm a little worried about Vanessa, dear. She would never tell us anything about her trip to London, save that she found it boring and could not wait to get back to us, and since I had already written to her Godmama, imploring her to say no word of the escapade to the Talbots, no harm was done. But this morning, I went into her room to take the new gown which the sewing woman had made, and . . . Oh, dear, Rhoda!'

To Rhoda's surprise, tears were trickling slowly down her Mama's plump cheeks. Rhoda jumped to her feet and took her mother's hands in her own, patting them kindly.

'Whatever is it, Mama? Don't say the naughty chit was rude and unkind to you again?'

'No, no, dearest, indeed not!' Mrs Mordred sniffed, dried her eyes on a wisp of handkerchief, and continued with her tale. 'She was standing before her dressing-table, in her wrap, and she had been crying. Of course, I pretended not to notice, but bade her slip her wrap off to try the gown on, and . . . and . . .'

'Now don't start again, Mama, tell me what's upset you,' her daughter coaxed, knowing full well that only time and patience would get her the whole story. 'Vanessa was crying, and . . . ?'

'Oh well, she turned away and I knew she was

wiping her eyes, and she turned back and slipped her wrap off, so good and patient dear — and so unlike herself! And Rhoda, she's so *thin!* I c-could see her little ribs, and there seems nothing of her! And . . . and so sad, Rhoda!'

'Thin? Yes, I thought myself that she hasn't been eating well,' Rhoda said slowly. 'Hardly at all, in fact. Often she slips most of her meal under the table to Curly. But . . . Oh, Mama, do you think she's ill? Has some sort of wasting sickness, perhaps?'

'I don't know,' wailed Mrs Mordred, tears welling up in her eyes once more. 'But I can't bear to see her so unlike herself! I thought she was such a difficult child, and so ungrateful and hard. But . . . but she was full of life, and always laughing, and now she's nothing but good and quiet, and I wish she was her naughty, difficult self, so I do!'

'Perhaps you ought to tell her so,' Rhoda said thoughtfully. 'I've had a bad conscience about Vanessa in a way, ever since she got back, and brought Curly. It occurred to me — and I don't know why I didn't see it before — that when I was a child I had kisses and cuddles from you, and from my Papa, and even affection from Charlie. But poor Van — well, Mama, I daresay it never occurred to you to give her a kiss now and then!'

'I can't say it did,' Mrs Mordred said, looking surprised. 'She's not a child, Rhoda my dear!

And anyway, you and Charlie have always been so good, so affectionate! I've never felt a lack of affection, though I'm a widow.'

'That was not what I meant, Mama,' Rhoda said patiently. Ideas, she knew, took their time to penetrate into her Mama's brain-pan! 'I have thought, lately, that it is Vanessa who may feel she lacks affection!'

'Why, how ridiculous, I am quite fond of the child. Indeed, when I see her looking so wretched and thin . . .'

She got out her handkerchief again and dabbed at her eyes.

'Don't distress yourself, Mama. I've noticed since her return from London, that Vanessa lavishes all her kisses and caresses on her little dog, and it seemed to me that she does so because you show her so little affection.'

'It has never occurred to me to do so,' Mrs Mordred said, surprised. 'She is immensely rich, Rhoda, or will be one day, and I never thought . . . that is . . .'

'Oh, Mama, all the riches in the world cannot make up for love! You *are* fond of her! Do show it!'

'Upon my word, the poor child! Of course I'm fond of her, and I *will* show it! I shall go into the garden — if that's where she's hiding herself — this minute, and give her a kiss!'

'Good. And then perhaps she'll grow a little fatter,' Rhoda said optimistically. She watched her mother trot from the room, then returned to

216

her needlework, but her mind remained with her cousin Vanessa.

Something had happened to Vanessa in London; something so important that she could not even bear to think about it, for sometimes she would see Vanessa in deep thought, a dreamy little smile playing about her mouth. And then, abruptly, Vanessa would jump up, call to her dog, or make an excuse to leave the room. And always, when she did so, her face would wear a stricken look.

Well, whatever it had been, it had passed, Rhoda thought philosophically now. Time cured all things, and soon it would be summer, and Vanessa would be her bridesmaid and take part in all the wedding celebrations. And then it would be autumn, and time to begin the preparations for her cousin's first Season with visits to the dressmaker, buying trips to the shops and excitements galore. Vanessa, she was sure, would be all right!

Vanessa, meanwhile, was wandering through the pleasure garden, walking alongside the drive where the rhododendrons were in heavy, purple blossom. She had Curly with her, on a smart leather leash, and if anyone had asked her she would have said she was walking her dog but in truth, she was doing what she did so often these days; passing the time.

She kept her thoughts resolutely turned from Jerome, but could not forebear to wonder, just a little, what Mathilda was doing. The season was well advanced and unless Mathilda was about to announce her betrothal, she would be home soon, or off somewhere with her fond Papa.

It was cool and quite pleasant walking under the trees, but presently she thought that she would prefer to walk along the drive. There would not be so many flies there, and neither would Curly keep stopping, in the infuriating way dogs did, to sniff at every single bush, tree and indeed twig, that they passed.

She turned aside and pushed her way through the rhododendrons, knowing that she was dirtying her yellow sprig gown and not caring one jot. It was much too big for her anyway; now that her appetite seemed to have deserted her, and her waist had shrunk away, no clothes looked nice on her.

When I've forgotten him, I'll make Mr Talbot buy me some nice clothes, and I'll start eating properly again, she told herself. She never used Jerome's name now, not even in her mind. It hurt too much.

She had turned back towards the house and was tugging the reluctant Curly behind her, when she heard the thud of hooves on the gravel. She glanced back, and saw a tall man on a black horse, thundering down upon her. For a moment her heart stopped, then she shook her head and walked on. Imagination, of course! How many times had she seen him, shopping in a crowded street, driving a coach, standing in a crowd? Yet always it was just a fleeting resemblance, never him in very truth.

'Vanessa!'

The horse was pulled to a halt beside her, and the man astride vaulted down and grabbed her, holding her close against his thundering heart. She dropped the leash and shut her eyes, standing inert in his embrace, not daring to believe the truth — that he had sought her out and was here, that she was in his arms at last!

'My darling!'

He began to kiss her; little, soft kisses at first, on her brow, her small nose, her cheeks. Then his lips moved, almost tentatively, to her mouth and suddenly her arms were round his neck, her body straining against his, and he felt her tears run down and mingle with their kisses.

When he suddenly held her away from him she felt deprived. She shook her head muzzily, to clear the daze of happiness, and said slowly, 'Jerome? You've come for me? It is me you want?'

He nodded, but his hands were on her waist, his expression one of dawning horror.

'My darling, what's happened to you? What have they done? You're so *thin,* so terribly thin! And so pale!' He gripped her tightly for a moment, speaking through clenched teeth. 'I'll kill whoever did this to you.'

'No one's done anything, I've not been eating much. But why have you come now, Jerome? Why didn't you come before?'

'Because I didn't know where you were! I hunted,

and asked, but I couldn't find you. And then Mathilda took pity on me, and told me you were the housekeeper's daughter at Bascombe Hall.'

'*Wha-at?*'

'Yes, she told me. I suppose she thought I'd change my mind but I knew it was you or no one. Vanessa, my dear, my only love! Will you marry me?'

Her eyes were dancing; suddenly she was the wicked, teasing creature he loved, and not the pathetic little waif he had held between his hands.

'I'd like to marry you, Jerome, but I doubt my guardian would allow it.'

'I'll talk to him! I'll tell him that I've considerable property . . .'

'It's no use, darling, Jer! You see, he'd say you were only marrying me for my money!'

'But you have no money! Nor have I, but we won't care a fig for that! Take me to the house now, and I'll talk to him.'

They had turned and were walking back towards the house, Terror following meekly, a rein's length behind, Jerome walking with his arm tightly clasping his love's thin shoulders.

'It would be no use. He would say, "You, sir are after Miss Vanessa Bascombe's fortune, and I want it for my own son!" '

'Miss — but you are Miss Norris!'

He stood stock still, turning her to face him. She shook her head, solemn-face, but her eyes were lit with laughter.

'No. I lied, my love! I'm Vanessa Bascombe

and I own all this . . .' with a gesture which included the great, brooding mass of the hall, the pleasure gardens, the estate. '. . . all this and a great deal more besides. Surely you've heard of the Bascombe heiress, Jerome?'

He nodded absently, but there was a look in his eyes which stopped her teasing and made her put her hand up to gently touch one lean cheek.

'Don't look like that, Jerome! There's always the border!'

She laughed up at him as the expression on his face changed to one of blazing, dangerous excitement.

'You'd do it? You'd fling your cap over the windmill and fly to the border with me? We'd be finished in some people's eyes you know, and some would say I'd only done it for your fortune, and some . . .'

She fairly hurled herself into his arms, kissing him wildly, saying: 'I don't care! I don't care for anyone, only for you! Oh Jerome, run away with me please! Let us go *now!*'

A small, plump lady had come out of the shrubbery and was standing a few feet away, watching them open-mouthed.

Jerome drew back a little.

'Is that your guardian? Should I ask her . . .'

Vanessa reached up, shamelessly kissing his lips until he stopped talking and kissed her too, all the hunger of the weeks apart burning between them.

'You mean it? Then up with you!'

He threw her up onto Terror's saddle then sprang up behind her and swung his mount to face the driveway once more. A wild yap from around Terror's hooves made Vanessa shriek: 'Jerome! Reach down for Curly!'

He was settled in the saddle with Vanessa cuddled safely into the curve of his arm but he leaned down, the dog leapt up, and then they were thundering down the driveway again, with Terror apparently indifferent to the double burden.

They turned out into the road and Vanessa sighed blissfully and laid her hand against Jerome's cheek.

'Where shall we lie tonight, my darling?'

He chuckled, and kissed the palm of her hand.

'Together.'

He tightened his knees on the stallion's sides and Terror obediently broke into a canter.

'You are wicked!'

'Not wicked. I just want to make sure of you, this time.'

They rode for a while in silence, both so content to be with the other that words were not necessary. Then Vanessa said: 'That was my aunt in the drive.'

'Really? I wonder what she thought.'

'Mm hmm. So do I.' She leaned back against his arm, giving a sigh of contentment. 'I don't care a jot though.'

'Nor I.'

The powerful stallion continued his steady

222

progress towards the border.

At Bascombe Hall, Aunt Nessie retraced her steps through the garden and back into the house where she found her daughter still working on her petticoat.

'Rhoda dear, you know what you said about poor little Vanessa wanting to be kissed?'

'Yes, Mama. Did you take my advice and kiss her?'

'No dear, I'm afraid I didn't. But I admit you were right.' Nessie Mordred turned puzzled eyes on her daughter. 'She must have wanted to be kissed very badly!'

'Oh? Why do you say that?'

'Because when I found her, she was being kissed by a tall dark-haired man I've never seen in my life before.'

'How strange!' Rhoda got to her feet and peered out of the window. 'What was the explanation? Where's Vanessa now?'

The older woman sat down in a chair and closed her eyes. 'I really don't know! Do ring for tea, dear, I declare I'm parched. She and that man jumped onto a horse he had by him and galloped off. I really felt quite vexed with Vanessa, for she did not even introduce me!'

'That was exceedingly thoughtless of my cousin,' Rhoda said, her voice scarcely shaking at all. Beneath her breath, she added: 'So *that* was what Vanessa did in London!'

We hope you have enjoyed this Large Print book. Other G.K. Hall & Co. or Chivers Press Large Print books are available at your library or directly from the publishers.

For more information about current and upcoming titles, please call or write, without obligation, to:

G.K. Hall & Co.
P.O. Box 159
Thorndike, Maine 04986 USA
Tel. (800) 257-5157

OR

Chivers Press Limited
Windsor Bridge Road
Bath BA2 3AX
England
Tel. (0225) 335336

All our Large Print titles are designed for easy reading, and all our books are made to last.